WHAT THE ... ?

Now, a bull calf of the Black Angus tribe is a perfectly fine thing to be … Not, however, when your previous experience of life has been that of a man! And this is the predicament in which I found myself.

BULL

A novel by FREDERIC SMITH

To my sweet wife,
with love,

Frederic Smith
6-24-14

AHWIPRIE
BOOKS

Bismarck, N.D.
www.ahwipriebooks.com

Cover art by Linda Stefanson Smith

$14.99
ISBN 978-0-9821700-5-2
51499>

9 780982 170052

$24.99 outside U.S.

Library of Congress Control Number: 2014901982

AHWIPRIE
BOOKS

P.O. Box 2673
Bismarck, N.D. 58502
www.ahwipriebooks.com

Dedication

To Linda's and my good children,

SAM, TOM and WIN

Also by Frederic Smith

The Baggage Room (novel, 2011)

BULL

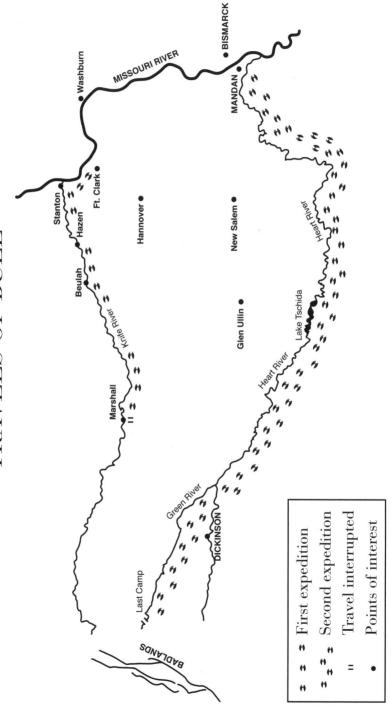

TRAVELS OF BULL

Washburn

MISSOURI RIVER

BISMARCK

MANDAN

Stanton

Ft. Clark

Hazen

Hannover

New Salem

Beulah

Knife River

Glen Ullin

Lake Tschida

Heart River

Marshall

Heart River

Green River

DICKINSON

Last Camp

BADLANDS

First expedition
Second expedition
Travel interrupted
Points of interest

CHAPTER 1

I was born in a barn, on a bed of straw, by electric-lantern light, two men attending. The barn creaked and whistled from the violence of the storm raging without, a spring blizzard.

As my thoughts came into focus, I was aware of something amiss. It wasn't a matter of pain; I just felt ... *all wrong*, somehow.

The older man was speaking words of comfort to my mother. "You're going to be fine," he coaxed. "And you've got yourself a fine baby boy."

I struggled to rise for a better look around. Swinging my head, I hit it against my arm. The arm was covered with black hair and had a hoof on the end of it. That's when I let out my first bawl.

The man chuckled and turned to his son, kneeling beside him in the straw. "A fine boy," he repeated. "Listen to the lungs on him, will you?"

Now, a bull calf of the Black Angus tribe is a perfectly fine thing to be — part of the Big Picture, no doubt. Not, however, when your previous experience of life has been that of a man! And this is the predicament in which I found myself — source of my loud complaint.

Moreover, I burned with the knowledge of how it had come about. It was the doing of my nemesis from a previous life — and, later, in the Happy Hunting Ground — a scoundrel by the name of Counts the Coffee. He had done it to me again!

* * *

My first days were difficult. Recycled humans are supposed to assume their new roles as blank slates, their memories wiped clean. In my case, this wouldn't have suited Coffee's purpose — which required that I suffer the knowledge of the dirty trick he had played on me.

I remember the day, the storm having abated, some of us new calves were let out of the barn and corral. The snow was melting at a rapid rate, exposing great patches of gray sodden pasture, and there was a lot of standing water. With my fellow youngsters I splashed and cavorted, forgetting my situation long enough to give way to a calf's natural playfulness.

Then, pausing to drink, I watched my image shimmer into focus in the gray water. This brought home more forcefully than all my bitter thoughts the cruelness of the trick that had been played on me.

My bellow of pain brought my anxious mother on the run to throw a bag of teats in my face. Poor Mother — she thought food was the answer to everything. I couldn't touch a drop.

Without knowing it, I touched bottom that day. Thereafter, things gradually began looking better to me. There was, for one thing, the sweetness of my mother. Barely graduated from girlhood — she had been bred as a 15-month-old — Mother shamed me by the gracefulness with which she assumed a role as new to her as mine was to me. I found her to be loving, patient, protective — and touchingly addled. She found me a handful.

In the matter of my name, I would not stand for her lovingly bestowed "Precious."

"What shall I call you, then?" she asked.

"Bull," I growled, getting way ahead of myself, for sure. But it was only a syllable to Mother, and her desire to please was such that she accepted it without question.

I was thoughtless enough to always be correcting her.

"Son," she might say, "there's some nice grass over yonder that nobody else has touched. Will you go over there with me?"

The poor thing, she wanted it badly, yet was unwilling to go unless I accompanied her.

I was weeks from being interested in grass for myself, but there was a bigger problem.

"It won't do any good, Mother. It's on the other side of the fence. You cannot get at it there."

"Fence?" Behind her soft, unfocused brown eyes she mulled over the concept. "But it is so soft-looking and green!"

"It's a perfect waste of time. You can go and see for yourself, but I'm going to stay here and play with Billy."

Billy, an especially high-spirited calf born the same day as I, was my best friend.

With meek submission, Mother bowed her head and resumed cropping the poor pasture grass. Her selflessness made me thoroughly ashamed of myself.

I said: "I'll go, if you want to give it a try. But you will find it is just as I say."

I fell in behind her gently rolling walk, pitying her excitement. When she arrived at the barbed wire, she stuck her head through, but everything within reach had already been eaten down to nothing. Her disappointment was lost in amazement at my prescience. "But how did you know?"

"Mother, we tried the same thing yesterday."

"Yesterday?" Still another foreign concept caused her eyes to glaze over. "What do you mean, 'yesterday'?"

She regarded me as a prodigy, bragging to her friends, "He is going to be a great man someday." ('Great man' and 'someday' gave her no difficulty, being intuitive to her mother's heart.)

The other thing I had going for me: Even informed by my human sensibility, I was still a bull calf, in good health and enjoying a natural animal exuberance. There was much sport with my little friends, starting with Billy.

"We are twins, brothers," Billy maintained, and I liked him too well to let him glimpse the gulf that separated us. Indeed, it was easy in his company to forget it even existed.

Being pure unencumbered bull, he naturally assumed leadership in all our games, including the mock battles that never would have occurred to me.

"All of these women belong to me," Billy would growl (not having the faintest idea what he wanted with them). "The country is not big enough for both of us."

With that, we began butting at one another, knocking our heads together until we gave ourselves headaches or one of us was thrown.

We also enjoyed taking on, together, all the rest of the bull calves, invariably driving them home bawling to their mothers. Then Billy would say: "See, there is nothing we cannot accomplish together. We will always fight side by side and win all our battles."

"What about the women?" I teased him once.

"We will divide them up," he said seriously.

It was also gratifying to watch, even through bovine eyes, the advancement of my first spring in, oh, 175 years. The country looked like home, which is to say western North Dakota. I missed the antelope, which in the old days would return by the thousands from their wintering, south, in the Black Hills; and the buffalo, which would leave the shelter of the river bottoms and spread out over the plains.

But the great wedges of game birds — the geese and cranes — did come back as they used to, their voices stirring an ancient thing in my new blood. The orange whips of the water willow began to freshen toward yellow, and one day they were full of redwinged blackbirds and their vibrant cries of "*Locoweed!*" Crocuses stuck up their heads of yellow and purple, and this too was high excitement.

But memory, which allowed me to savor these things, also contained a barb.

For it was also at this time of year that my old people, the Mandan Indians, quit the wooded bottoms of the Missouri River they shared with the buffalo and returned to their summer towns on the bluffs. Indeed, I made this immemorial move with them on the last spring of my Earthly existence.

All gone now, that people and way of life — as vanished as the buffalo! All my years in the Happy Hunting Ground had not been enough, apparently, to wholly reconcile me to the idea, which now brought a lump to my throat again.

Perhaps now is the time to acquaint the reader with some of these memories and with their bearing on our story.

CHAPTER 2

I was born, about 1775, in one of our earth-lodge towns, Yellow Clay, on the east bank of the Missouri River. The Mandans, as we are known to history, were farmers and buffalo hunters. Our name for ourselves translates to "First People," which (I have since learned) is the approximate name by which almost every tribe, of every race, in the history of world has identified itself. (We can't all be right, can we?)

There are supposed to have been seven or eight thousand of us in a half-dozen of these towns in the Heart River neighborhood of the future Bismarck and Mandan, in North Dakota. I came along too late to remember such strength and security — only five or six years old when the first smallpox hit, taking off four-fifths of us in a single summer.

That's the picture I carry away from those days — of the loss of my parents, of death and despair on every hand. Then our good friends the Sioux discovered our plight and did their best to finish us off. They hung around our towns, killing anybody who left the safety of the walls to try to tend garden or go hunting. They even destroyed the gardens whose produce they were used to trading for in the fall. So, after a while, everyone left alive in our stricken towns was starving.

Finally, the worst of the disease ran its course — I was one of the few who never did get sick — and the Sioux had to leave on their fall hunt. With the pressure off, the survivors elected to remove upriver and set up near our allies the Hidatsa, at Knife River.

We badly needed the safety of numbers; besides which, our old towns were little but reeking cemeteries. The Sioux burnt them when they returned, imagining they were hurting us. But we were done with those places and their painful memories.

We consolidated into two new towns. I was still an East Sider, growing up poor in the house of relatives. But a good life was still possible even in those reduced days for a young man with ambition. I distinguished myself early in war and in the chase, becoming a man of some prominence, Black Bull Medicine. I married a West Side girl, taking her away from a man called Counts the Enemy, and went to live in her town, on Cross Timber Creek.

That's where we welcomed Lewis and Clark on their way up the river; and those worthies liked us well enough to winter over, with their party, in the woods nearby. Our corn helped see them through a brutally cold few months. I'm proud to say that Lewis and Clark were dinner guests in my house — and again on their way home from the great ocean a couple of years later.

A good life, as I say — although increasingly filled with white goods coming up the river first by keelboat and then by steam packet. We needed the white man's guns, because the Sioux had them, but much of the rest — blankets, metal tools and cookware — merely displaced what we were used to making for ourselves. And some of it was pure junk. All those beads and bells and little hand mirrors — it made me ashamed to see grown people making fools of themselves over these things.

I was one of the holdouts, a mossback. I tried to point out how all this *stuff* was pulling our lives out of shape, making us chase the buffalo more than we used to just for robes to give the trader. We were like a dog chasing his tail, I said. I could have saved my breath; for all the good I did, I was one of those dogs myself.

Finally we went to the length of moving a few miles downstream — abandoning our perfectly good houses and building everything anew — so as to be right beside the trading post, the future Fort Clark. I think the trader was fit to be tied; if he had wanted us right next door, he could have built at Cross Timber Creek. But what could he say?

I opposed this move, but the pro-white faction, led by Counts the Enemy, carried the day in council.

My old rival had been a good man once. Now all he wanted to do was hang around the fort and suck up the trader's coffee;

hence his nickname, which was gaining wide circulation, Counts the Coffee. (Later he would switch to firewater.) The trader cultivated him for help in getting his own way with our people.

The substance of our debate:

I: "What you propose is degrading, plain and simple. You are leading us down the road of weakness and dependence."

Coffee: "Why don't you ask the people if they would rather be degraded by poverty or prosperity? In any case, it is idle to rail against change that is already here."

We hadn't seen quite all of his change yet. Some fifteen years after our move, the annual steamboat from St. Louis arrived with a case of smallpox on board. The whites did their best to keep us off the boat, but in the confusion of unloading someone was able to sneak on board and steal a blanket. He snatched it right off the bed of the sick man!

Soon the traders came up to the town looking very grave. They explained the danger, offering five good blankets for return of the bad one. Either the culprit did not believe them or he didn't want the name of thief over something so small. Anyway, he did not come forward. Our soldiers searched every house, but the blanket could not be found. Finally the whites returned to the fort, shaking their heads.

When the first case of putrid fever — our name for it — appeared a month later, it was in the house of Counts the Coffee.

It was the nightmare of my childhood all over again, as the disease swept through us like a fire, taking off ten or twelve a day at its height. It turned your flesh black and rotted it on your living bones. We danced, we prayed, all to no avail. Soon there weren't enough healthy people to tend to the sick or to bury the dead. The bodies just had to lie there. People lost all hope and began killing themselves, jumping off the bluff onto the rocks below.

It was the effective end of us as a people. It came as a great relief to me when I awoke with a headache one day and knew

I would be out of it in a day or two. My wife and three of our grown children had perished already, and the heart had gone quite out of me.

My surviving son said, "Father, we will meet again in the other world."

To comfort him, I agreed, although doubting it in the pain and distraction of my heart. Could the Great Spirit who had proven himself helpless to save his First People deliver on the promise of a Happy Hunting Ground?

CHAPTER 3

Foolish doubts! I awakened, as promised, to a joyful reunion with my wife, children, parents and others who had gone before. Ironic that we should then mourn the absence of that last boy, who not only survived the smallpox but lived to an advanced old age on the reservation!

I was not long in making myself at home, having passed other intervals in the HHG, and renewing many old friendships. Some, like that with Meriwether Lewis — and with William Clark, who would join us in only a year — dated from one Earthly existence or another. Others had been conducted exclusively in the spiritual sphere, interrupted by our separate and several journeys into flesh, during which we never met (and would not have known one another if we had).

A new feature since my last visit: a newspaper by which residents kept track of Earthly doings. I was reading in it one day the discouraging account of the spread of the smallpox to all the northern tribes, and commenting on it to Lewis, when my friend sat taller and exclaimed:

"Surely that is our old friend Counts the Enemy coming down the street!"

So it was, although I don't know how Lewis knew him after all this time. It had been thirty years; besides which, Counts the Coffee had since discovered a fondness for the food kettle that rivaled his regard for the coffee pot. The old lineaments were badly blurred — or, perhaps we should say, overlaid.

He was looking around him as he walked, a self-satisfied smirk on his overfed mug, when Lewis sprang up and rushed to seize him by the hand.

I was embarrassed for my friend. Lewis had died years and years ago, and word of Coffee's transformation had not made it all the way up here.

"And, if I am not mistaken, there is Black Bull Medicine!" said Coffee, eyes glittering with mischief.

Ignoring him, I said to Lewis: "See how long it has taken

him to find this place! He died six weeks before I did."

Coffee shrugged. "So I took a couple of wrong turns! I am here now, the same as you."

True enough: In the HHG we're all thrown in together, the bad with the good, just as we were on Earth. The 'why' of that I leave to the theologians. (We have those up here too, but even they confine their questions to one another, nobody tasking the Great Spirit himself.)

"I do not understand," Lewis said. "Surely the two of you are the same as when I left you, equal in honor and with voices that are loud in the council?"

"Sir," I corrected him, "you see before you the wickedest of men, a false prophet to his people for selfish gain and the direct cause of their ruin."

I filled him in on some of the particulars, Coffee listening with impatience.

"You want to watch what you step in," he advised Lewis. "Our people ceased to regard the ravings of this fanatic years ago. They understand that their future lies in accommodation of the white man's superior magic.

"Talk about false prophets! The people renounced this one, and it has made him crazier than ever."

I made a move at him, and Coffee sought shelter behind Lewis.

"There remains," Lewis said coldly, "the fact of their unhappy fate. For them, the future of which you speak is no more. Or were you aware that, of all the Mandans, only a handful survives?"

"Is that a fact?" Coffee clucked. "Well, that is most unfortunate! Also unavoidable, if you take the long view. The future was not with them in any case. Just look around and you will see what I mean."

Keeping Lewis between us, he took in our surroundings with a sweep of his arm.

"I appeal to Black Bull Medicine — is this the Happy Hunting Ground of which our fathers spoke? And what is that thing you are holding there in your hands?"

True, the HHG had added, since my last stay, more new features than just a newspaper. There were oil lights, water wells, horse-drawn streetcars — all kinds of marvels to dazzle a poor red man. That's because the Great Spirit is the father of more children than just us First People.

I *am* able to say that — even as my dear wife has insisted on something more up to date for ourselves, and we now make our home in a modern bungalow — the Great Spirit has chosen for his own domicile one of our traditional earth lodges, favored for its coolness in the summer and because it is proof against mosquitoes.

Also, for all that the streets here bustled with modernity, at the ends of them — where the city gave way to country — there were still buffalo on every hand.

Coffee denied being able to see these at all. If he was telling the truth, what was there to say to a man as blind as that?

I said: "A traitor could never hope to find the home of his fathers. I am content that you have worked the last of your wickedness on Earth, and that this place is secure against even the likes of you!"

Nevertheless, I was made uneasy by the sinister chuckle with which he answered these words, and I saw Lewis frown darkly. Coffee saw that last too, and must have divined he no longer had an ally in that quarter.

"We shall see," he said coolly, withdrawing, "whether a good man will not land on his feet wherever he finds himself! Gentlemen, I bid you good day."

Lewis and I watched his departure, my friend commenting, "There goes — if not the wickedest of men, as you call him — one who is certainly up to no good."

Coffee had not gone half a block when we saw him fall in with some cronies from the old days at Fort Clark and disappear through the batwing doors of a saloon.

Lewis said, "He will bear watching!"

CHAPTER 4

To return to twenty-first century Earth and my four-legged adventures:

In May our owners, named Dolan, moved us to new pasture on the other side of the road. This offered a view of their mailbox and suggested a way of getting a better idea of my whereabouts.

Mrs. Dolan was a great 'go-er.' The men also often being busy elsewhere, the mail — which appeared mid-morning — was seldom claimed until lunchtime, earliest. So I picked my spot, and excused myself to Mother one morning.

"You are not to worry," I said. "I will be gone for only a few minutes, and you will be able to keep an eye on me the whole time."

"I don't like it, son," she fretted. But, poor thing, I had her so wrapped around my finger, so to speak, she could refuse me nothing. "But remember — no talking to strangers!"

"Mother, I am only going about fifty feet."

That distance had no more meaning for her than fifty miles, and I left her half-sick with anxiety.

I squeezed under the fence and crossed the road. It was no trick to open the mailbox with my teeth and extract the mail. I read with a start of joy the legend across the top of the newspaper: *The Bismarck Tribune.* Not only was I back in North Dakota, as I had suspected; the Dolans' address was Hannover, which put me no more than thirty-some miles from my old town beside Fort Clark!

Had Counts the Coffee meant to tease and frustrate me with this proximity, so near and yet so far? I cared not, walking around for the rest of that day in a happy dream. Come what may, I knew I would somehow find the means to revisit my prior Earthly home and commune with the scenes of a vanished time.

This was not my last visit to the mailbox. Soon, in fact, I had renewed my newspaper habit from the HHG and especially my fondness for the syndicated columns of one Ed Advancing Along.

Advancing Along, whose mug shot showed a handsome American Indian of middle years, was a brother spirit in more ways than one.

You could liken the country's finances to an eating disorder. We Americans have binged on public money until we can barely waddle around, digging our economic grave with our teeth.

The Congressional Budget Office says that in only 11 years, by 2025, "entitlements" and interest on the national debt will consume every last federal tax dollar. That means no money for "discretionary" niceties, such as the national defense, that we don't borrow.

Few Americans understand their monetary system, and who can blame them? However, the one thing everybody should be able to understand now, with the example of a bankrupt Europe before them, is that there is an end to affordable credit at last — a time of accounting when people will pay dearly for their self-indulgence.

And their government will not be able to save them — us. We will be lucky, for the sake of public order, if some semblance of government is able to save itself.

One windy day the paper got away from me, and I'm afraid that what got put back little resembled the original. I thought I had better lay off the next day, and sure enough, there was Mrs. Dolan out to meet the rural carrier.

I listened with some embarrassment as she complained of the sogginess and generally disreputable condition of her mail in recent days.

"It's almost as if someone had been slobbering on it," she said.

The mailman took heated exception to this interpretation, and they parted with bad feeling on both sides. Realizing that a little self-restraint was in order, I gave up my newspaper for a few days and was always more careful with it thereafter.

This excitement was as nothing compared to that of the day Buster the bull got out.

Buster was my father, Billy's father, the father of all us calves that spring. He was a great ugly brute with shoulders like a hill who lay for hours every day in the trees across the road, chewing his cud and daydreaming of his next love affair. Mother never acknowledged his existence by word or look. As dim as she might be about most things that happened to her, Buster she remembered.

Buster's time was coming — the Dolans started breeding their cows in July — but a storm of wind and rain one night threatened to accelerate the schedule.

A fallen branch made a gap in Buster's fence. When we rallied at the water tank next morning, he was standing in the road, studying us.

Mother was beside herself. Her big eyes rolled and she started to bolt, the first time she had ever forgotten me long enough to think of herself.

I blocked her way. "Listen, Mother — you will only call attention to yourself. You must stay where you are, among the others."

Nodding miserably, she assented, although trembling in every limb. Another of the cows, brighter than she, said, "Anyway, there is still the fence."

I set no great store by our fence. The wood posts were mostly rotted off at the ground, leaving the barbed wire to stand more out of habit than anything else.

Still, it looked for a while as if everything might be all right. Buster seemed as paralyzed as we by the turn of events. He had his freedom, but didn't know what to do with it. Maybe he had been on his July schedule for so long that he thought May was only for planning.

He stared at us, massively immobile, for minutes. Then he swung his great boulder of a head to take a swipe at some roadside grass.

It figured that, if something was going to upset this delicate

14

equilibrium, it would be my reckless pal, Billy. Fearless himself, and too young to consult the general weal, he bawled out in his cracking adolescent's voice:

"What's the matter, Grandpa? Forgotten where to put it?"

Somebody must have gotten next to Billy with some rudimentary knowledge. He was shushed immediately, but the damage had been done. Buster's tail shot straight up, and his bellow of rage sounded louder in our ears, and a lot more personal, than the thunder of the night before.

"Now we're in for it," quailed a yearling steer. "What did you have to open your mouth for, you little brat?"

"Aw, what can he do?" Billy shot back.

Buster wasted no time in showing us. Lowering his head, he charged into the ditch and came boiling up the other side, hitting the fence in full career and sending the posts flying like clothes pins. Wire enveloped him like a cloud, increasing his fury while scarcely slowing him down.

It was utter panic. Cows, calves and steers scattered in every direction — all save Billy, whom I saw (out of the corner of my eye, as I fled with Mother) standing his ground, albeit pawing a trifle nervously.

But Buster was after bigger game than a two-month whelp. He passed Billy and, as I had foreseen and feared, took after us. Poor Mother, what few wits she had thrown into helpless confusion, headed for the worst place, a blowhole in the side of a hill. There Buster cornered us; and, as she cowered against the earthen wall, bellowing, began cuffing her with his head, trying to turn her around.

He was the mightiest living thing I had seen since my buffalo-hunting days, when I had been better armed; and, slavering and roaring as he was, made a fearsome spectacle. However, my outrage was stronger than my fear, and I lit into his backside with all my puny strength, giving him a shot where it would do the most good.

His cry of pain and anger was terrible; then he was coming down on me like an avalanche. I sidestepped his charge and took off in another direction. Buster would have quickly overtaken me if he hadn't stumbled and gone down on one knee. Mother, perceiving the threat to her little darling, rallied heroically, charging and dealing him a mighty clip.

Buster was staggered; and then brave little Billy waded into the fray. The two of us fairly danced around him, tormenting him from two sides, until he couldn't decide whom he was madder at; while, every time he threatened to get organized, Mother would deal him another blow.

As spent, finally, as angry, Buster ended by telling Mother she could "just keep it — and much good may it do you!"

Then he noticed Billy's mother, who had followed her son and remained standing on the sidelines.

This had Billy and me ready to do battle again. But Billy's mother said, "Why don't you boys go someplace and play nicely for a while?"

Buster was out of luck here, too, as just then the Dolan men came bouncing up in their pickup. It was almost possible to feel sorry for the brute as he was herded back across the road, leaving five tracks, as they say.

CHAPTER 5

The life of a stock animal offers dramatic illustration of the principle that there is no such thing as a free lunch.

The Dolans had a classical cow-calf operation. At about three months, the male calves are subjected to an operation that keeps their wants simple and food-directed. Then they are called steers. These may be sold off, to a feedlot, as early as fall. Others may be fed at home into the winter, awaiting an uptick in the feeder market; some even enjoy a second summer on the grass. One way or another, they usually finish eating their way to slaughter by twenty months, latest.

The girls — heifers — have it easier, some always being retained to replace cows whose best breeding days are behind them. If they make good calves, they may be kept around for seven or eight years, until their own reproductive machinery falls into decay. Then, of course, they go to market too, there being no retirement homes for menopausal grandmas.

We had a few yearling steers on the place that spring. They were a dull lot — narrow where they should have been broad, and vice versa — and a source of wonderment to Billy.

"They never want to play or go exploring," he observed one day. "What is the matter with them?"

I explained that they were older than we — practically grown up — and had put away our childish notions of fun.

"If that's the case, then why aren't they interested in the women, like Buster over yonder?"

You see how engagingly smart the little rascal was. "They aren't that old," I lied bravely, but it sounded lame even to me.

"Huh!" Billy snorted. "If you want my opinion, I don't think they will ever be like Buster. Just look at them — all they ever want to do is eat! You and I will be like Buster. Why, even now, if I was a little taller, they wouldn't need that big dummy around here at all."

Buster's abortive raid had indeed put ideas into his head, and he had begun making a nuisance of himself with our little girlfriends. The results had been comically incomplete to date, but he was on the right track.

Passing in their truck one day, the Dolan men paused to watch and smile.

"That one is certainly advanced for his age," I heard from Dolan Sr., to which his son replied, "I guess he'd better have his fun while he's able, right?"

This was in June — exquisite, soft season for humans, a hard one for bull calves. I knew only too well what the son was getting at, and that the time was drawing near when, if we wanted to keep what we had, Billy and I would have to run away.

I confided none of this to my friend, thinking it kinder not to burden him before the event — a grievous mistake. The truth is, I was scarcely reconciled to the idea myself. The prospect of having to say goodbye to Mother began to weigh on my every waking hour.

The change did not go unnoticed by that dear dim creature who was so acute where her boy was concerned.

"Son, you are not yourself," she observed daily, and would question me minutely about my eating and bowel habits. Satisfied that my health was in order, she always finished with the same gentle joke.

"You act like someone who has got himself a girlfriend," she teased.

It was at moments like these that the weaker side of my nature whispered, "Submit." After all, I was a bovine, for all practical purposes; I had no idea how Billy and I were to get along on our own in the wide world. Staying here, we would be subjecting ourselves to no worse than awaited all our fellows. And I would be buying precious time with Mother — long summer days under soft skies that would be only slightly less sweet because I could see ahead to the end of them.

Then I would picture Counts the Coffee on his malevolent cloud, rubbing his hands and chuckling as I went under the knife, and it renewed my resolve to be a bull and free. It was personal, yes; but it was also in my mind to strike a blow, however small, against Coffee's evil work, which was not confined to the HHG and to cattle pastures, as I will show later.

* * *

It's common for ranchers to combine the tagging, branding, vaccination and castration of calves into one operation. This takes many hands and remembers the old days, when so much farm and ranch work was done cooperatively. The neighbors get together and move from place to place, working the calves.

Accordingly, I was always on the lookout for a suspicious gathering of men. Also, I took to crossing the road after dark every night and eavesdropping through a window on the Dolans' conversation. My vigilance was rewarded one night, a Tuesday, when Dolan Sr. hung up the phone to tell his wife:

"That was Emil. We start with his calves at eight in the morning. He's real light this year, and we should have time to do the Klingenschmidts', too."

"When will you be over here?"

"As of now, day after tomorrow."

"Thursday," Mrs. Dolan mused. "I'll have to have ice cream and some of my shortcake."

Ice cream and cake!

I hardly slept that night, and wandered around next morning, which was very hot, in a red-rimmed daze. I could hardly bear to look at Mother. What could I say to her, when I could find no words of comfort for myself?

I took Billy aside after lunch.

"Look here, my friend. You know those adventures we have always talked of having one day? It is time to start on them — tonight!"

He was all eagerness and curiosity, taking special pleasure in our slipping off after dark. "Just so we are back in time for our midnight snack!"

Milk from our mothers, that meant.

"No midnight snack for us, Billy."

I could have deceived him, but he did, after all, have his own goodbyes to say. His eyes grew large, and he shook his head in disbelief at what he was hearing.

"What? Run away and never come back? Never see our mothers again or any of our friends?"

I couldn't help it — my head hung miserably, and tears filled my eyes.

"That is a strange idea of fun, I must say!" Billy said indignantly. "Why should we want to do a thing like that, when there are plenty of adventures to be had right here at home?"

After much vain argument, during which I tried to convince him of the superiority of those adventures that lay "out there," I broke down and told him the rest of it.

Billy snorted. He shook his head some more. He didn't believe me.

"Now I know you have freaked out for sure! The very idea! Why, if they tried to pull anything like that on me —"

He made a ferocious face and tore at the ground with one hoof. I was getting desperate.

"Look, Billy. You know those steers that you despise, that you are always making fun of because they never want to play or chase after the women? They were not always like that — they used to be the same as you and I! Then they had the operation, and you see what has become of them."

He stopped his pawing, and uncertainty briefly entered his eyes.

I hurried on: "You can see those tags they wear in their ears. Haven't you wondered why they have them and we don't? They got them when they had the operation!"

He thought about this for a moment, then chuckled in a sly way. "Ha! If that's what the tags are for, then what are all the women doing with them too?"

Talk about being too smart for your own good! Before I could explain, our attention was diverted by the nickering of a horse.

Now, the Dolans kept no horses. I turned with Billy to discover not one but a half-dozen of them coming slowly with their riders down the road.

Billy didn't know what to make of these fabulous creatures, half beast and half man; he stiffened and took a silent step forward, all systems on alert. I was uneasy in my own right — apprehension that changed to alarm when the first horseman turned in at the approach to the gate. Then the Dolan pickup came into view, loaded in back with more men laughing and talking.

There had been a change of plans, and they were coming after us a day early!

CHAPTER 6

We had made it easy for them by gathering beside the well, across the road from the farmstead. Most stood shoulder to shoulder in one large body — a favorite bovine strategy on the hottest days, don't ask me why. Billy and I were off to one side, in the same blowhole where we had vanquished Buster.

Half the horsemen fanned out on our perimeter, the others — along with the men on the ground — taking up positions by the gate or on the road. The idea was to cut out the calves for a short walk across the road to where the work was to be performed in a pair of corrals by the barn.

It did not take Mother long to find me. "I don't know what this is about," she said. "But you must stay close to me, just in case."

I tried to concentrate on Billy. He had never recovered from the appearance of the man-beasts. Like a weathercock he stood, helpless and dumb, unable to take his eyes off them and impervious to my pleas.

"You see, it is happening just as I said!" I cried. "You must come away with me now!"

"No, no," Mother said. "What is this you are saying? Your place is here with me. I will take care of you."

The riders tightened the circle around the main body, yipping and nudging it toward the gate. Yearlings and cows were encouraged to slip the noose. A few mothers, however, stuck with their calves. The serious unhappiness started when the first one was shunted aside at the gate and her calf hustled through. She commenced a frantic bawling — *Uh-ruh! Uh-ruh!* — a cry quickly taken up by others.

Billy and I had not escaped notice. The nearest rider, the rest of his cattle in motion, wheeled his horse about and started for us.

This was it. Fighting down the emotions that threatened to immobilize me, I told Mother: "Dear, I must get out of this. I will return to see you when I can." Then, to Billy: "Brother, this is our last chance. Let's go!"

I gave him a butt with my head, trying to break his trance. But he merely shifted his feet and resumed his statue's pose. I gave up and, shutting my ears to Mother's bawl of despair, made for the fence.

I just beat my horseman there, squeezing under the wire. "Why, you little son of a gun!" he exclaimed, drawing up. He must have expected me to be stopped by the idea of the fence. He turned his mount and started back the other way.

I had a minute — nobody else was paying attention to me. I stood and watched as he closed in on Billy and Mother, and gave a last despairing cry:

"*Bill-y!*"

They were swept away.

I turned my back on it all and took off running north up the ditch. I ran until my lungs were on fire, the most sustained all-out effort of my young life. My eyes were a film of dirt and sweat, my ears stopped with the thunder of my blood. Say that I was not the most sensitive instrument, just then, for the recording of information. I galloped up an approach and just got the brakes put on before I could run up against something blocking the way on top.

The Dolan pickup.

I had never heard or seen as it overtook and passed me on the road above. The son looked down at me from the passenger side, smiling. It was the smile of a farm boy who knew from Sunday school that man has been given dominion over all the animals and who was amused at a challenge to that authority. He opened his door and started to get out.

I scrambled for the road with all my remaining strength. My progress seemed to me nightmarishly slow, and I expected to feel at any moment the clasp of rough hands. But I made it to the gravel, and across, plunging down the other side.

Still free!

I heard young Dolan laugh, and sneaked a look over my shoulder on the fly. He had crossed the road on foot and was moving away from me at an angle that cut off further flight to the north. Straight ahead was a shelter belt that paralleled the road back toward the farmstead. It was several rows deep and grown tall with grass and weeds. I darted in, thinking I might conceal myself long enough to at least catch my breath.

Young Dolan was smart, cutting all the way through the belt to the pasture on the west side — thus preventing my flight in that direction — then turning south to drive me before him. He also gave himself easy walking, while I had to plow through fallen branches and undergrowth. His dad, meanwhile, had turned around to pace us in the pickup on the road.

I was able to take an occasional breather, which I hoped might fool the boy into passing me on the outside. No luck with that, however; when he couldn't hear me moving, he stopped too.

Eventually I was at another crisis, with light showing through the trees where they ran out at the Dolans'. I stopped, at bay, on the fringe of the belt, no more than a hundred yards from the barn. Before me, the men were walking the calves down the driveway toward the barn and corrals. Behind me, it sounded as if young Dolan had quit the pasture and was moving in the belt now.

In extremity, and for the first time in my new incarnation, it occurred to me to pray. It was, of necessity, a silent prayer, addressed to the Great Spirit of my Mandan fathers, and I worried it might not get through. The Mandans gave their maker no credit for mind reading, their communications with him tending to be clamorous in the extreme.

In this case, shouting could not have produced results any faster. For I had scarcely lifted my eyes toward the heavens when the means of my deliverance was shown me in the branches of the Siberian elm under which I stood.

Now, I know cattle are not supposed to be able to climb trees — although it's possible that none ever needed to as badly as I did. I also know that the Great Spirit can do anything he wants, and give him all the credit.

My tree was squat and bushy, after the habit of the species, its crotch at about shoulder height. I made a great leap, fairly knocking the wind out of myself — but I stuck. Then, when I had recovered my breath, I gathered my legs under me and clambered to the next landing, making the tree shiver in every branch and leaf. And lay very, very still.

When young Dolan came up a couple of minutes later, he passed right under me. He walked to the end of the belt and scouted around on the outside, calling to his father, on the road, "Have you seen him?" Then he returned to stand only feet away, puzzling, looking and listening.

I don't know how he could have missed the beating of my heart, which sounded so loud to me.

"Let him go," called the old man. "He'll come home when he gets hungry."

Young Dolan shrugged and started for the road.

Grateful as I was for my escape, the ensuing hours were a trial. I was afraid to leave the safety of the tree by daylight, although my perch grew exceedingly uncomfortable after a while, then painful. Worse, from there I was forced to listen to the business being transacted out of sight in the corrals.

The calves kept up a constant affrighted clamor, punctuated with sharper cries when one of them got the branding iron or the knife. Every so often I caught a whiff of singed hair and hide. The sounds of distress were just as loud from the other side of the road, as the mothers, hearing all, reacted to what must have sounded to their ears like a massacre.

Allow me to say at this point that I do not mean to represent these proceedings as cruel or inhumane. Temporarily uncomfortable for the animals, yes — in the same way that human children are sometimes made uncomfortable by the necessary ministrations of parents or doctors.

But I assure you that most stockmen — certainly including the Dolans — feel at least as tender toward the poor brutes by which they make their living as does the casual sentimental observer, and inflict the least discomfort consistent with the job. The discomfort is, in any case, of short duration; and, a few hours later, the calves and cows remember about as much of it as you and I do of last night's bad dream.

No, the pain I felt was mostly on behalf of Billy, that bull calf with a difference. Because I could not distinguish one voice from another, every bawl from the corrals might have been his, causing me to suffer along with each until the work was done at last.

CHAPTER 7

The men finished by late afternoon, but that was not the end of my "treeing." After they had returned the calves to their mothers, they retired to the house for their refreshments. Even when that broke up, and the last pickup and horse trailer were on their way, I felt I must stay put — stiff and sore or not — awaiting the cover of darkness.

The sun set at last, bringing up its opposite number, a full moon, to sharpen its image over the east pasture. The robins wound down their vespers; nighthawks twanged like arrows, invisibly, in the dusky air. The cattle, wrung out by their exercise and by the emotions of separation and reunion, settled down early, big shapes by small. One cow alone kept up her dirge in the blowhole beyond the water tank.

After the way of summer nights in North Dakota, it cooled off as soon as the first stars were out. I dozed, waiting for the lights to go out at the Dolans'. When I opened my eyes, the moon had climbed a couple of degrees and the house was dark. It was just the crickets and I, and a tree frog ringing on a sad minor note.

I half-climbed, half-fell out of the tree, scuffing myself up but not breaking anything, and crossed over to the pasture. Almost everybody lay about like statues in the blue moonlight. I tiptoed among them, for there was one I dreaded meeting even more than Mother. Of course, he was the one I came on first.

I sensed someone watching me, and turned in time to see his eyes reflecting the moonlight. He closed them immediately, feigning sleep, and this told me he wanted an interview as little as I did. He was giving me the opportunity to pass him by, which out of consideration for both of us I might have done, had I thought him really asleep. As it was, we were committed to one of those rites of pain the rules require of us from time to time.

"Billy, I've come to say goodbye," I said, standing over him.

His ears — one bearing the brand-new ID tag — flattened stubbornly on his head, although he would not open his eyes or acknowledge me in any other way.

"I'm sorry," I told him — and could not think of anything else to say. We were beyond words now. Fierce, proud and shamed all at once, he pretended to the end not to hear, even as a single tear betrayed him, escaping from under a closed lid to run down his cheek.

I touched my forehead against his and took my leave.

Mother was standing vigil where I had left her, head nearly touching the ground. The poor thing had fallen asleep on her feet. As I watched her, heart filled with pity and love, and wondering if the kind thing wouldn't be to leave her as she was — she awoke.

She was all over me, moaning and chiding. As she told me what she would do to me if I ever dared run off again, she was licking me all over. Discipline had never been Mother's long suit.

"Mother, I must go away again this very night."

I explained that the Dolans would be looking for me in the morning; and how, as the only untagged calf, there would be no hiding out. "You heard that commotion across the road this afternoon. You cannot want that for me."

She nodded even as her head drooped lower and lower. Then, pushing her powers to their limit, she had a bright idea. "Surely you could take me with you!"

I explained why that wouldn't work: If we were discovered together, no matter how far from home, the brand on her flank would be our ticket back to the Dolans. And she accepted that too. We huddled in the moonlight, shedding tears.

At last Mother's practical maternity asserted itself.

"Have you thought about how you are going to live? You still need your milk, no matter how grownup you think you are!"

She made me promise to look up a nursing cow every day for at least one square meal. "They will be happy to help you, if you are nice and polite about it," she said, and then her face clouded over again.

"Mother, what is the matter now?"

"Oh, I am so wicked, I don't like to think of anyone feeding you except me!"

Do you see what I mean about obligatory pain?

But it was Mother's loving attention to duty that got us over the hump, she insisting that I eat before starting out. She said nothing about a "last meal," and I put the thought out of my mind. We were learning.

The feeding was comforting for both of us, I think; I certainly felt better afterwards, more confident about everything. A full stomach is usually an optimist.

When we nuzzled goodbye, I promised her that we would be together again one day, no matter what it took.

"I guess you can do anything you set your mind to," Mother said bravely. "I know you will make me proud."

With that benediction, I was off to make my way in the world.

CHAPTER 8

Counts the Coffee did indeed, as he had predicted, "land on his feet" in the HHG. He started modestly enough, catching on as a file clerk in the Dispatching Office. "A fitting occupation for a warrior of his renown," Lewis mocked, and proposed a new nickname: Counts the Paper Cuts.

Sixty, seventy years later, the laugh was on us.

Dispatching is the most important office in the HHG, responsible for the appropriate placement of resident spirits in new bodies on Earth. 'Reincarnation' captures the basic idea. Coffee's rise in Dispatching was so gradual — a pace consistent with his laziness — that none of us paid much attention. Finding himself, after five or ten years, pushed another modest step up the ladder, he would consolidate his new position by installing an old crony here, a new drinking buddy there — and send feelers up above, to the next rung.

If an overture were rejected, he quietly withdrew it and tried elsewhere. He made few enemies, did nothing alarming or flashy. To this day I think he was just trying to make himself comfortable as he went along, Coffee-style.

Lewis was the first to become alerted, way ahead of anybody else.

My friend and I toiled in Culture and History, which office squared with our interests but was not exactly a hot spot of influence. Coffee it was who introduced influence to the HHG.

One day Coffee moved up again, acquiring one of those titles that is twice as weighty as the job duties. 'Second secretary to the third deputy' of something or other — I couldn't say the whole thing without my eyes glazing over. I sought out Lewis immediately, my appetite whetted for one of his sarcasms.

I found him, instead, in a black mood. I did get the sarcasm, though.

"You are amused?" he asked, giving me a smoldering look. "Why, friend, if disaster is your dish, you must have laughed your head off when the Titanic went down last year!"

To say I was taken aback is an understatement. Rather than explain, Lewis commenced an agitated pacing, his occasional exclamations intended not for my enlightenment but for venting of his distress.

"Oh, oh, oh!" I heard. And, "Folly — absolute folly!"

After my initial shock, I couldn't help finding this behavior comical and a little absurd. "But Lewis — second secretary to the third whatever," I prompted.

Lewis fixed me with a look that had the glaze of fever — or worse.

He said: "I learned of the appointment last night. From that hour until this, I have exerted all my influence trying to get it reversed. People I have counted friends for hundreds of years — none will help. They laugh me off — like you — blind to the danger fairly jumping up and down in front of their eyes!"

There was more in this vein — none of which, I am ashamed to say, I was able to take seriously, except insofar as it appeared to reflect unhappily on the stability of my friend.

Here it must be said: For all his brilliance and customary good humor, which ordinarily made him the best of companions, Lewis had a morbid side. This expressed itself in periodic depressions so severe that one of them may have accounted for his mysterious Earthly demise, at an inn on the Natchez Trace, in Tennessee, in 1809. Suicide — that was the whisper one heard; although Lewis' story was that he had been done in by an intruder, a burglar.

I asked William Clark about it one night, in the frankness of our cups. He looked as if he would like to have said something, before putting me off with, "You must take that up with Lewis." Which of course I never did.

Another manifestation of Lewis' dark side was a sensitivity to conspiracies that nobody else could detect. It was to this I initially attributed his ravings about Counts the Coffee. My own hatred of Coffee had entirely to do with the harm he had worked on Earth. He was still a self-seeking wretch, to be sure; but just as surely, Earth was now out of his reach and the HHG simply beyond his competence for mischief, even if he was still so inclined.

I persisted in this complacency until it was quite too late.

Next, Lewis quarreled loudly and publicly with Sgt. Charles Floyd of Expedition fame, who had committed the sin of accepting a modest position under Coffee.

"I always suspected he blamed me for my failure to provide a physician on our journey," Lewis told me afterward, "although he never said a word to me until now. The scorpions I discovered when I turned over that rock! He insists I cheated him not only of his life but of his fame."

This came as a surprise to me, who had always regarded the two as fast friends. Floyd, of course, was the only man lost on the Expedition, from the "bilious colic," when it was only a few months old. His grave, however, was long ago rescued from obscurity and is marked today by a soaring obelisk in Sioux City, Iowa, overlooking the river.

"Coffee offered him the job in order to spite me," Lewis continued, "and the traitor has accepted it from the same motive. I'm only sorry that I allowed them to see how well they have succeeded."

This break with Floyd, as well as succeeding manifestations of his fixation, disturbed others besides myself — notably, Mr. William Clark.

Clark, who temperamentally was as different from Lewis as day is from night — steady where Lewis was erratic, plain where he was poetic — was hard-pressed to conceal his impatience. The two had been working on authorization, from the Great Spirit himself, for another great Voyage of Discovery, to the planets this time. Clark viewed Lewis' behavior as detrimental to that effort.

"He's making us a laughing stock with his persecution of that Coffee buffoon," he complained to me.

They finally had words over it, and it was sad to see their relationship, once so warm, become merely correct. Clark eventually took a different partner for the great enterprise —

which, however, failed, being forced to turn back at Mars. His genius was meant to work in tandem with Lewis', as Lewis' with his. Separately, the spark that had provided greatness was gone.

Lewis was beyond caring about such projects, unwilling to relax his scrutiny of Counts the Coffee. These were years of isolation for him, during which I was one of his few outlets. I was there to hear "I told you so" when Coffee, promotion following promotion, was elevated to Number Two man in all of Dispatching.

By this time Lewis was so starved for vindication that he fairly rubbed his hands as his forbodings were realized. "I hope Number One has his affairs in order," he chuckled.

Number One was a gentle, virtuous soul and an optimist about human nature — the sort of lamb who would admit a wolf to the fold if he smiled prettily and flossed between meals. Lewis thought Coffee was his personal affirmative-action project.

Six months later he disappeared, leaving a letter Coffee dutifully offered to the press.

"I hope I may be forgiven," it read, "for seeing my opportunity on Earth and seizing it somewhat ahead of schedule. I leave the Office in the capable hands of my trusted lieutenant," etc.

Lewis characterized it as "the suicide note of someone who has been pushed off a tall building." Which experience at Coffee's hands — an unceremonious dispatch — I was of course to suffer myself one day.

CHAPTER 9

More will follow on the sinister career of Counts the Coffee. For now, it's back to Earth and my flight from the Dolans' — toward, if I had known, worse danger than I had left behind.

Leaving Mother, I set out north again up the Dolans' road. I was gratified when, in a mile or so, this 'T'd out,' continuing as a pair of mere ruts on the section line. This promised remoteness, for a ways, from farm houses and the dogs likely to awaken them.

My goal was nothing less than my old home at Fort Clark. This was more than just sentiment (although I badly wanted to see what was there today). I was counting on some woods on the bottoms in which to hide while I thought out some kind of future for myself.

A look at a map of North Dakota will show how, starting from the Hannover neighborhood and keeping north, I could not fail to find either the Missouri River or its tributary Knife. From there I would be able to walk into Fort Clark blindfolded.

My grassy track served me for miles, crossing a couple of gravel roads but encountering no houses. Sometime in the wee hours, I breasted a height of land and plopped down for a breather. The view was impressive — moon-drenched country extending for miles on every side — and I was feeling pretty satisfied with myself.

Mother, when I thought of her, was still an ache; however, more of my thoughts were, of necessity, forward-looking now. If Mother was far behind me, so were the Dolans, who would never think of looking for me so far from home. Now I only needed to avoid falling into the clutches of somebody else — which I proposed to do by traveling at night, hiding out by day.

I had it all figured out — or so I thought.

My hill made part of a long east-west ridge that ran out of sight in both directions. Gazing idly along its western profile, I saw something I hadn't noticed before, a gray shape in the moonlight. I took it for a rock. The thing was, when I took my eyes off it for a minute, then happened to look back — the rock had moved. It appeared closer now, and offered besides a couple of disturbing features: prick ears and pale, glittering eyes.

I scrambled to my feet and made a run for it.

If my legs hadn't already been so busy, I could have used them to kick myself all the way down the hill. Wandering across the prairie in the light of the full moon as if I hadn't an enemy in the world! What had I been an Indian for, not to know any better than that?

Mr. Coyote seemed in no hurry, just loping along and driving me before him, as if to let me run myself out. I looked at him over my shoulder: He was grinning in a not-unfriendly way. It was as if he was not all that hungry and was enjoying a little sport before dinner. A coyote can be playful as a cat that way.

From the bottom of the hill the chase continued on the plain. I thought that, if I could only find the right kind of tree, I would show him some sport he had not bargained for; but there was none offering. I did see ahead an arrangement of three big rocks that offered protection for my back, at least, in a last stand. I made for them, Mr. C. clicking his teeth at my heels.

There I wheeled about and brandished my front hooves. Mr. C. stopped a few yards away, flashing me a smile that said as well as any words, "Let's see how long you can keep this up!" Truly, it was a stance I could maintain for only seconds at a time, and whenever I touched ground again, he inched a little closer.

Also, I had no real striking power with my front legs. My best hope, if I could anticipate his final rush, would be to turn and give him a good shot with my hindquarters. Of course, if I missed with that, it would be quickly over.

A queer sight our little duel must have made there in the moonlight! Mr. C. had nearly closed the distance between us, and I was showing him my hooves again, when one of the rocks moved behind me, pitching me forward into his very jaws!

Startled, he jumped to one side. I landed beside him on my knees, utterly at his mercy and expecting at any second to feel his teeth at my throat.

Instead he stood stock-still and looked over my shoulder, one lip curled quizzically. Played out, unable to even think about moving, I looked back too.

One by one the three big white rocks grew legs and stood to a great height against the stars. The first bull — the same I had chosen to protect my rear — lowered a head the size of a bushel basket and made the ground shake with his roar.

"What are you doing," he thundered, "bothering this miserable little piece of veal? Don't you have any appetite for steak?"

This was addressed to Mr. C.; who, far from having ambitions in that direction, quailed at his words. Then the other two bulls moved up in support, and he slunk away with ears flattened and tail between his legs, casting back at me a regretful look.

Trembling, I regained my feet and looked dumbly up at my terrifying benefactors. They were the first white cattle I had seen, of a tribe known as Charolais.

"And you, you little black puppy," the first one rumbled. "Where did you come from, and what do you think you are doing, running around at night by yourself? You'd better tell us the truth, or we might just decide to eat you ourselves!"

They all rumbled in appreciation at this little joke, moving in until I was quite surrounded. I felt as if I were at the bottom of a deep gorge, gazing up at the cliffs. Still, I managed to blurt out the story of my flight, to which they listened at first in astonishment and then with sympathy.

"I have always wondered where steers came from," nodded the first. "Men, we are in the company of a brave and enterprising lad."

Then, turning back to me: "But you must give up this

nighttime business once and for all. The country is crawling with coyotes just now. You are way ahead traveling by day and taking your chances with the Two-Legs."

I promised to do as he said. Then, as if reading my mind, my new friend said: "You will need a place to rest and get something to eat. Follow us."

Grateful and weary, I accompanied them on a short walk to the first fence, from which we could see a considerable gathering of ghostly white cattle by a grove.

"Ask around for Bertha," said my gruff but kindly mentor. "Tell her Duke wants her to fatten you up some. And tell her this."

Chuckling, as much for the benefit of the others: "Tell her, if she will come around at moonrise tomorrow night — fence or no fence, I will return the favor."

"And bring a couple of friends," said one of his companions, and the three of them stood there rumbling and shaking with mirth.

It had been a long day, the most harrowing and exhausting of my life; now, at the end of it, when it was time to thank and say goodbye to these unlooked-for friends of my own kind, I got all choked up.

"Go on," Duke said impatiently, giving me a rough boost toward the fence. "And take care of yourself until you are big enough to — take care of yourself! We need fewer steers and more bulls."

CHAPTER 10

I was hospitably received by Bertha, a big milky creature for whom a recommendation by "the Duker," as she called him, was sufficient, no questions asked. She was nursing a calf of her own, Duke's son; but, as she said, "Honey, I've got enough of this stuff to open a store." I filled up until I could hardly move, then curled up for several hours of restorative oblivion. Waking around noon, I tapped Bertha a second time and, with thanks, took my leave.

"Honey, you were no trouble at all," she said, and nodded toward where her son was raising some devilment with the other calves. "Not like that one over there. He's a chip off the old block, for sure."

Sadly, that was no longer true. He had already been "fixed," and would be settling down, becoming a solid citizen, soon enough.

Bertha was only the first of several cows on whose kindness I imposed, as the trip I had originally envisioned as a lark of two or three nights turned into something rather more extended. I simply couldn't cover the same ground by day, slowed by the heat and the wider detours I had to make around farm houses. The detours also confused my sense of direction; I missed having the stars to steer by.

Coming to my rescue here were the great tall smokestacks of the coal-fired power plants that, I knew, had gone up in our old Mandan neighborhood. When I worried I might be going wrong, I just found a height of land and got my bearings again.

I chased those stacks for days. Finally, by first light one morning, I struck what I took for river hills. But there was something wrong with them — they were too smoothly contoured, too perfect, with no rock litter and no trees or woody plants growing in the draws. They looked as if they had been made yesterday instead of in the last glacial epoch.

I got a panicked feeling I had gotten lost somehow and was

not where I was supposed to be. I began to hurry. Panting, I topped a last rise — and stopped cold.

In the United States, you do not absent yourself from a place for even five or ten years and return expecting to find it physically unchanged. I had been gone for rather longer than that. On the one hand, I could recognize my old river valley — the very scene before my eyes — in broad outline. It was where the Missouri drops down past modern Stanton and the mouth of the Knife River, and bends east for an extended run to Washburn. The pretty bluff opposite the Knife has the same woods at its base as it did in my day.

But the view immediately below where I stood was otherwise, overlaid with industrial development. There are two power plants, taking up — along with their coal stockpiles, tipples, conveyer systems and switchyards — a couple of miles of riverfront. Radiating out from them, ranks of tall steel towers march toward the horizon, transmission lines slung over their shoulders in silver webs. There are railroad tracks and a highway.

I sighed for old pastoral ways even as I recognized the inevitability of their passing. The valley here had been a magnet for human commerce since before the coming of the white man, when we were a big native trade center. Today the action is lignite coal, a great and practically inexhaustible natural resource. Those funny hills I had just navigated were nothing less than the earth put back by human agency after the coal had been pulled out from under it like a rug!

Clearly the old neighborhood was not meant to live quietly, in the afterglow of Lewis and Clark. Why, the very river is a different color — blue instead of the old brown, most of the silt now settling out of it behind a dam fifty miles upstream.

I dropped down the hills to the bench and thence to the highway, which was quiet this early. Crossing that, I picked up the railroad, which also followed the river east.

Now, on the home stretch, didn't my excitement mount as the old and familiar peeked out at me from under superimposition of the new! The first power plant, belonging to Great River

Energy, occupies one of our townsites, final home of my old East Side people, after they had been forced to cross the river and join the rest of us for protection from the Sioux.

A stubborn and independent lot, the East Siders; they are that way to this day in the HHG. This intrusion by the whites, building on their very bones, has not been taken kindly. Many is the time, in the HHG, I have seen them dancing themselves into a frenzy, making medicine against the boiler or electrostatic precipitator.

A hint to the power-plant people: A modest gesture to the old inhabitants, such as renaming your plant something like "The Black Cat Indian Village Station," would do your cause a world of good, leading to fewer breakdowns and turnarounds.

A trestle took me over Cross Timber Creek, where we hosted Lewis and Clark. The site has been under cultivation, besides having been cut into by the railroad and highway, and there is little to see now but pottery shards and animal bones. This made me feel sad, and I passed on after only a few minutes.

I give the white settlers and state of North Dakota credit: The site of our town at Fort Clark, at which I arrived shortly, has never gone under the plow, and is preserved today, along with the site of the trading post, as a state park, a grassy plot of two hundred acres.

The setting is classical, on a promontory protected by steep banks on two sides. We closed the triangle with a ditch and palisade and were virtually unassailable. In the distance, mercifully undisturbed by mining, are the beautiful folding hills depicted in the paintings of George Catlin and Karl Bodmer (like Lewis and Clark, houseguests of mine).

But you can ask only so much of grass; and, at first glance, the grounds look like nothing so much as idle pasture. Of our old cemetery, which lay outside the walls and that I came to first, not a trace remains. Of course, this was not your white man's cemetery, with graves and markers.

We called it "the place where the dead live." We wrapped a body in robes and placed it on a scaffold, where it remained for years. When the scaffold fell at last, the skull was retrieved and placed in a circle of other skulls belonging to the family.

This allowed the dead to visit among themselves and also made them accessible to the living. On almost any day you could see people there among the skull circles, talking with departed loved ones. It was all very homey; the women would bring their sewing and make a day of it.

Today, all gone — the last scaffold long since rotted into the ground, the skulls carried off by souvenir hunters a hundred years ago.

I took encouragement when my feet found the remains of our old palisade ditch. It's only inches deep now, instead of feet, and narrow where it once was wide. But one hundred and seventy-five years have not succeeded in effacing it — prompting the odd reflection that, if you want to build for the future, only dig a hole in the ground.

Likewise with our old houses, vanished themselves but their floors remembered by a hundred circular depressions. Long compaction by vanished Indian feet has caused a different variety of grass to grow up in these than in the intervening spaces, showing them off to good advantage.

I wandered among them, lost in a dream of the history they represented and of which I had made a part. Now it was all quietness and tall grass.

From the point of land I saw that the river had retreated by a mile or so, and so long ago that great trees had had time to grow up in its former bed. Some of these raised their crowns above the very bluff, and in them I heard calling one to another the descendants of the birds I had listened to in my former life.

There was a corrective for human vanity for you. Our religion instructed us that the Great Spirit had made the Fort Clark neighborhood, if not the whole world, with the Mandans expressly in mind. He might as well have hung out a sign.

Turns out he made it for the birds!

I'm not picking on my poor vanished people. There are plenty of folks who believe the same kind of thing about themselves today — that they have been singled out for the

41

Great Spirit's unique blessing. They don't all wear feathers in their hair, either.

I had allowed myself, as you can see, to drift into something of a funk. Homecomings can be like that, especially when you're all by yourself and there's nobody to help you validate what used to be true and real; to confirm that everything isn't just the dream it all seems now.

What saved the experience for me was the inspiration to look up my old house.

In every one of our towns, the most prominent families had their houses arranged in a cluster toward the river side. I was practically standing there already; it only remained for me to align myself with the tip of the promontory and count house rings.

I knew I had the right one from the surge of energy that went through me as soon as I stepped inside. It was my humanity coming back to me. Over this very spot had moved my family in the daily rounds of life — our very footprints preserved only inches down, beneath the grass of years, in the dust of the earth as it had used to be!

This rush of identification and feeling was like a flash of lightning, and could not be sustained in its original brilliance. But it had done its work, showing me the needful perspective.

Counts the Coffee had been our next-door neighbor. I visited his house now. It looked nearly the same as ours, but was implicit with his unique and obnoxious presence.

In his memory, and with all the maturity of a months-old calf, I went to the bathroom in it.

CHAPTER 11

Earlier I said that my aim in fleeing the Dolans' was not only to preserve myself intact but to frustrate, in however small a way, the "evil work" of Counts the Coffee. It's time I elaborated on the doings of that villain once he had installed himself as top man in Dispatching.

He started with a purge, top to bottom, of his known enemies, as you would expect. Waverers were given a chance to absorb the message and get with the program. Most did. Replacements, and the new hires with whom he began to plump up the payroll, came from the growing ranks of Coffee sycophants in the general population.

In only five years he doubled the size of the bureaucracy. Coffee justified this bloat by the press of business. "One quarter of all the people who have ever lived are alive right now," he told the newspaper.

Dispatching being the office to which all good bureaucrats deferred, Coffee critics became hard to find in other departments. In Culture and History, I had the mistaken idea I would bring out a history of the Mandans with a concluding chapter on Coffee's perfidy.

My boss, a decorous soul, was horrified when he saw the proofs. These were destroyed, and I received my walking papers, on some trumped-up grounds, not long thereafter.

Because of his prominence, they could not just tie a can to Lewis. They could, and did, deny him a publishing outlet, save for the letters section of the newspaper, that lonely forum for the rabid and disenfranchised. Not only did Lewis' increasingly angry broadsides light no fires there; they allowed Coffee to reply in tones dignified and statesmanlike. Lewis finally gave them up as counterproductive.

"That's all right," he said. "I wasn't telling half of what I know, anyway. I'll save my ammunition until I have enough to blow him to Kingdom Come."

Kingdom Come — isn't that where we were suppose to be already?

In fact, this was at the heart of the problem. In the HHG, it was simply not possible to foment the partisan fervor at which Lewis aimed. The best people were otherwise occupied, with long thoughts more appropriate to the spiritual sphere, I suppose.

Lotus eaters, Lewis called them.

In this permissive and inattentive atmosphere, Coffee was able to manipulate his office in the most cynical fashion.

Patronage — his construction of a huge and self-serving political machine — was the least of it. More serious were the changes in age-old policy. These were never advertised, but word would occasionally leak to the public. If there was a stir, which rarely happened, Coffee would be there with another press release, blowing smoke. As here:

From time immemorial, souls performing honorably in a previous Earthly life had been rewarded with favorable placement in their next. As a notable example — all did not follow so straight a line — George Washington made his return as Dwight D. Eisenhower.

Under Coffee, that was out the window. He argued that this kind of "privilege" was "unacceptable," denying opportunity to those who, for one reason or another not their fault, had been unable to burnish themselves to so high a sheen. From now on, souls would supposedly queue up for pot luck.

This sounded fair to the undistinguished majority in the HHG, even as people began to suspect that for preferment by merit had been substituted preferment by Coffee. As one restroom scribbler had it: "It's like smoking a good joint. The harder you suck, the higher you get."

More than ever, people competed to bring their loyalty to Coffee's attention, while refusing to criticize him even in private conversation. Anyone might be a spy, and he was rumored to have bugged all the public gathering places.

Lewis claimed to find, over time, an impact on Earthly affairs, including those that concerned him most, in the United States.

There he deplored, as the twentieth century advanced, the growing size and intrusiveness of government, almost a mirror of Coffee's Dispatching. A series of Cold War leaders, including presidents, seemed flummoxed by the Soviet Union and its proxies in Korea, Vietnam and finally our own hemisphere. As the 1970s advanced, even the American genius for prosperity foundered in shortages, inflation, high interest rates and unemployment.

Everywhere one looked, up or down, the good seemed to be in retreat.

Well may one ask: Where was the Great Spirit in all this?

The Great Spirit was an elusive physical presence; I never made a sighting, myself. But, if one were to judge from the sounds emanating from his earth lodge, he had become a huge fan of country music. I'm talking Roy Acuff, Wilma Lee and Stoney Cooper, Ernest Tubb — the real hardcore, addictive stuff.

One expansive night, Lewis offered this conjecture:

"The drowsiness of old age is upon him. It began when man, his favorite creation, kicked off from the nest, choosing freedom and death over his smothering love. (The Garden was the original welfare state.) Although he must laugh up his sleeve sometimes to see how eagerly people will turn around and accept the overbearing supervision of other men!"

Lewis himself seemed more and more resigned to the drift of events. News that would have been worth a fit before — such as Coffee's promotion of Sgt. Floyd to chief of staff — now elicited only a sardonic chuckle.

The sun burst through briefly for him in the mid-1970s with the emergence of Ronald Reagan as a presidential hopeful. "One has slipped through the net!" Lewis cried, and for a while was his old self, bristling with observations as he hadn't for years.

Then, just as quickly, the sun disappeared again as Reagan lost out at the 1976 Republican convention. Now the pall was worse than before: Lewis actually took to hanging out in the

Skid Row district, to all appearances one with the sodden characters with whom he had taken up.

His special friend was a particularly malodorous-looking fellow in rags. The two of them could be seen nearly every evening lounging against a wall under the streetlight, passing a bottle back and forth.

Finally I intercepted Lewis one night as he weaved home from one of these meetings.

"My dear fellow!" I protested. He looked a wreck; however, his breath, as he wavered in my face, was clear of any trace of alcohol.

"Bear with me a while longer!" he whispered, even as he threw off my arm and resumed his unsteady course.

I would have bet money on his sobriety. Of his sanity I could not be so sure — but, then, that had been the case for a long time.

Finally he appeared at my door one night, freshly shaven and laundered and in a state of high excitement. He carried a briefcase. This proved to be crammed with official-looking papers. He grabbed a handful and brandished them before my eyes.

"It's all here!" he cried. "Documentation of his malfeasance from Coffee's own files!

"Here's Mark Twain — a dangerous man to have looking over your shoulder, you will agree. Coffee sent him packing the day he arrived! For a lifetime he has been scratching in the sand with a stick in the jungles of the Amazon.

"Abraham Lincoln is licking food stamps in California."

Lewis cited case after case, any one of which would be sufficient to topple the Coffee regime. "I have an appointment with the Great Spirit himself at ten o'clock tomorrow morning!"

Dazzled, dazed, I asked how he had come into possession of this evidence.

"Do you recall the ragged fellow I like to hang out with in the paper-sack district?" he laughed. "That is Coffee's good right hand — and, unbeknownst to him, my left one — Sergeant Charles Floyd!"

"He has been with you all along!" I cried.

"From the day he went to work years go and we arranged that spurious quarrel. Of course, neither of us guessed at the time that he would rise to a position of such usefulness."

Lewis enthused: "I tell you, with Reagan on the ground — I'm assured he *will* be president one day — and the Great Spirit back in effective charge up here, there is reason for cautious optimism about the future.

"Tomorrow tells the tale!"

CHAPTER 12

I tossed all that night, my sleep roiled with bad dreams. Waking for good at seven o'clock, I found it had clouded overnight. A few drops of rain blew in at the window, and the streetlights still glowed in the murkiest gray light. Was this a proper beginning for a new day for heaven and Earth?

Lying abed for some time, I tried to tell myself that my dreams were shadows out of the past, and that the long nightmare of Coffee's reign was almost over. Still, I remained full of unease. What if something should happen to Lewis and his evidence before his meeting with the Great Spirit?

I had begged Lewis to allow me and some other friends to pass the night with him; he had refused on the grounds that any such suspicious gathering was bound to be reported to our enemy. Rather, he made me promise not to leave the house until I heard from him again. "I must know where to find you," he said.

I rose at last to dress and fix myself a small breakfast — the beginning of a long morning of waiting and worrying. My wife was away, visiting relatives, and there was nothing to distract me from my anxious thoughts. I paced — and peered out the window at a day that continued gloomy and unseasonably cold. A sullen dripping began that looked as if it had settled in for all day.

Ten o'clock came and went.

Finally, at eleven-fifteen, there came a knock at the door. I was there in a bound. Standing in the rain was not Lewis, however, but a sullen-looking stranger with the lapels of his coat turned up around his face. Mutely, he held out an envelope.

"Who are you?" I inquired, taking it. But he turned without a word and stalked off down the street. Behind him lingered on the air a fruity bouquet of drink. I looked after him, puzzling, until he turned in at an alley and disappeared.

I tore open the envelope. It contained a handwritten note,

scrawled in apparent haste: *Come at once. He wants to see you too. — L.*

That explained the messenger, I thought: He was one of Lewis' tatterdemalion irregulars. I threw on a raincoat and hat and plunged outside into the mizzle and gloom. Perhaps my testimony was needed for corroboration of Coffee's Fort Clark career, which Lewis knew only at second hand. My nerves fairly hummed, and I found myself wishing I had taken more pains with my dress. The prospect of coming face to face with the Great Spirit was daunting; I hoped I would not be too rattled to give a good account of myself.

The earth lodge came into sight, a wisp issuing from the smoke hole on top. This homey detail, suggesting that even the Great Spirit could get cold in his bones, requiring a fire for relief, reassured me somewhat.

(The hole was partially covered, Mandan-style, with a bullboat, to keep out the worst of the rain. Nobody, so far as I knew, had ever seen the Great Spirit up on the roof, actually making the necessary adjustments; it was thought he was able to manage these by mind control. "Easy for him," my wife sniffed, in talking me around to our bungelow.)

The Mandan earth lodge is built of cottonwood logs covered with sod. One enters via a covered passage that descends into the house proper. At the bottom is no door but a partition of upright logs that shelters the occupants from drafts and prying eyes.

Approaching down this entryway, eyes already beginning to sting from the smoke, I listened for voices, but could hear nothing but the pulse in my ears. I drew up in front of the partition — still straining, still listening — and rapped on it shyly.

A voice, more amiable than not, pronounced clearly, "Come in, come in." It was a voice like any other; I don't know what I had expected.

Entering, I was brought up short when I could see nobody about. In the center of the room, in a pit, burned our traditional fire, spitting in the rain and giving off our traditional smoke (to which I had grown unaccustomed). Otherwise, the Great Spirit had made rather free with our old arrangements.

The dirt floor had been carpeted. To the right, where we quartered our best horses at night against theft by the Sioux, was a small kitchen and dining area featuring a table with two chairs. (Was there, then, a Mrs. Great Spirit?) On my left: a waterbed.

In back, along the wall where our beds of buffalo hide would have been, were a large desk and, beside it, one of the first big-screen TVs, dark.

"Lewis?" I inquired, for I hesitated to pronounce the sacred name.

"He has just stepped out," came the same voice as before — which, on my second exposure, sounded almost familiar. The smoke was getting to my eyes, and I continued to peer about vainly for the speaker. Perhaps the Great Spirit was *all* spirit, a disembodied ghost? But why then the necessity of a fire and other comforts?

"You will pardon, I hope, the ruse of the note," the voice continued, in a caressing fashion. I jumped as a highback chair, facing the desk with its back to me, swiveled about.

"I had to make certain that you would come."

My scalp prickled. Grinning up at me from the depths of the chair, face a ruddy death's head in the glancing illumination of the fire, was Counts the Coffee!

CHAPTER 13

Coffee laughed at my discomfiture. I hadn't seen him in years, and he had grown even fatter over that time, evolving this massive torso atop which his head sat as an excrescent afterthought, with features. His spindly limbs might have been gathered up by somebody else and thrown into the chair after him.

Like a gigantic bagpipe, that's what he looked like, wheezing laughter his song.

"You are thinking," he said, dabbing at his eyes, "that I am the record of my excesses. This is true! However, do not count on a stroke or pulmonary embolism to carry the day for you. I assure you, my life expectancy is quite as good as yours — in fact, considerably better!"

He lapsed into another fit of coughing laughter.

The loathsomeness of his person, added to the moral revulsion I had felt for him since our Fort Clark days, helped bring me to myself.

"I suppose you are the Great Spirit now," I sneered.

"Oh, my dear man, no," Coffee said, getting himself under control. "That is — not yet! You find me merely enjoying the accommodations. But that's right" — he snapped his fingers, as if recalling himself — "you did come here expecting to see *him*, didn't you?

"What a shame that your visit should coincide with his little holiday! I managed to convince him only yesterday that he really did owe himself. Here he is last night, in Nashville."

He fingered something in the arm of his chair, activating the TV. The big screen hurt the eyes with its burst of rainbow images, which proved to be musicians dressed in costumes that would have done an Indian proud. Even with the sound muted, it was easy to conclude that a country show was in progress.

"Now," Coffee said, as the camera quit the stage in favor of a pan of the audience. It zoomed in on a little old woman with blue hair.

51

"You're not telling me —" I started.

"In disguise, of course."

The screen went dark, and Coffee turned back to me, the fire now our principal source of light. The effect was quite primitive.

"You're the second one I've had to disappoint this morning," he croaked. "That is, our mutual friend Mr. Lewis also came here expecting to see the Old Man and not me. But," cocking an eyebrow, "I expect you know all about that. And about this."

He gestured casually over his shoulder, and I saw it lying open on the desk — Lewis' briefcase!

The blood rushed to my head, and I made a lunge for him around the firepit. Coffee raised a hand, and from it leapt a bolt of blue lightning, which he instantly recaptured and held, crackling and darting, in his palm. His expression had changed from a leer of patronizing cordiality to one rather more severe.

I drew up, and stood before him shaking with anger and astonishment.

"I surprise myself!" he exclaimed — and, smiling again, watched the shrunken bolt play and flicker in his hand. "I've never managed anything half so good before." He looked at me steadily. "I hope you will be warned, and not attempt anything impulsive again."

"What have you done with Lewis?"

He waved the question aside. "In good time, in good time. In the meantime, if you would be good enough to give me a little room."

I retreated to a place beside the fire, trying to impose calmness on myself even as my thoughts whirled. One of our old hunting spears hung as a decorative piece on one of the central posts that held up the roof. I was willing to make an attempt with it, whatever the cost to myself. But could I do any damage? For that matter, could I really be hurt by that pet lightning that tugged at Coffee's hand like a dog on a leash? I didn't know.

"That's better," Coffee said. "Regarding Mr. Lewis, you will be glad to know his visit was not wasted. I was quite as interested in his documents as our friend with the blue hair would have been!

"Of course, I could not allow such — what shall I call it? — prejudiced data to come before his eyes. It is, I am afraid, subject to misinterpretation."

"No interpretation required," I snorted, "to hang you by your stones, if any, from the nearest lamp post."

Coffee clucked. "By the friends of privilege and reaction such as yourself, perhaps. You overlook that my policies have found favor with the great majority, who are helped by them rather than not.

"If I had wanted to take my chances against Mr. Lewis' roguish eloquence, I think I might have justified them even to the Old Man! What's wrong with a clean slate and fresh start for everybody? A redistribution of the talent and the luck?"

"Like Mr. Twain in the rain forest, or wherever you stuck him?" I rejoined. "Save that stuff for the newspaper, Coffee."

His face darkened at revival of the name some of us had pinned on him at Fort Clark and by which nobody, I am sure, had had the temerity to address him in years.

I went on: "If fairness were really your game, you would be in over your head. If life isn't fair — if fairness is beyond the competence of the Great Spirit himself — how would a hack such as you manage it?

"But your game is otherwise — patronage. You are like those Earthly politicians who put a thumb on the scale to create new winners and losers. In the process, they harvest votes, position and wealth for themselves, while the people study dependency and spiritual impoverishment.

"Look at yourself — how you have practically withered away in the service of mankind!"

Brightening again, Coffee shook with rich enjoyment, activating the folds of fat that hung over his belt.

"You reactionaries!" he laughed. "You were all born with

golden tongues, but you lack the common touch. You go on beating your heads against a wall, growing fewer and more haggard every year, because you refuse to recognize and credit what the people want. And the reason you won't face the facts is — they go against your principles!

"Oh, you are a high-minded lot, chasing and devouring your own tails for lack of better nourishment!"

There was so much of depressing truth in this — while being, of course, unresponsive to the original argument — that I was at a momentary loss.

"This reminds me of the old days," Coffee continued complacently. "Always: What do the people want? Or, the way you would frame it: What *should* they want?

"You think people are full of high aspirations and yearning to breathe free. I say, most of them want the basics of life, acquired with as little exertion as possible, plus their fair share of whatever extra is enjoyed by people who work harder, or were just born luckier, than themselves. And the rest of it can go hang."

"You are describing cattle, not men," I countered — a remark that, in the light of subsequent events, might have been infelicitous.

"Cattle," I said, "have never risked comfort, property or their very lives for the sake of freedom, as people have done. But to be up to the task, people need leaders who hold up to them, and keep before their eyes, a vision of what is good and true.

"Tyrants such as yourself, on the other hand, appeal to the base and selfish in them. You do this to make them low and animal-like — the only condition in which they would consent to be governed by the likes of you!"

Coffee sneered: " 'Low and animal-like' — that's your real opinion of them. And that's why you and your kind are in retreat all over the world."

"I do not flatter them," I said. "But, then, I am not constantly steering them toward the public trough, as you do. There is contempt for you!"

54

We glared at one another across the gulf that separated us, Coffee relenting first with an indulgent sigh.

"How you can play that old contraption!" he smiled. "Really, I wouldn't have missed it for the world. Yet — no offense — you are little better than a kazoo next to Mr. Lewis' symphony orchestra. I can see I was wise in not allowing him to make his presentation to the Old Man.

"Our leader has a soft spot in his head for oratory. 'Give me liberty or give me death!' -- he has a reading of that by the late Senator Everett McKinley Dirksen that he breaks out from time to time."

"Lewis," I said, recalled to my original concern. "Which was it for him — as if I didn't know!"

"Now you are being unfair," Coffee pouted. "You know that my business is dispensing life, not death!

"In truth, Lewis was overdue by some years for recycling. If I kept him around, it's because I found him stimulating — he kept me on my toes! And he was good! Planting Sergeant Floyd in my office — he fooled me completely with that one."

"Sergeant Floyd?" I inquired, innocently.

"Dispatched!" Coffee thundered, and brought a fist down on the arm of his chair. "Gone this very morning, just like Lewis!"

A knot exploded in the fire, sending up a shower of sparks to illumine his hate-twisted face. "Will you see him? Do you want to learn what has become of your great friend Lewis?"

The TV picture came to life again as a mysterious room of subdued lighting in which a half-dozen baskets were set. I had to reach back in my readings to identify the nursery of a modern hospital.

"Look sharp!" Coffee snapped.

The basket at the end of the row, our target, turned out to be an incubator. We zoomed in, and nausea clenched my stomach with a hot hand. Within the plastic bubble, a tiny red human form was under siege, its limbs jerking with an uncontrollable agitation. The head lolled, and a hundred expressions twitched across its face. Worst of all were the eyes, which looked up at us with an adult calmness and clarity that belied the body's storm.

"The poor thing!" Coffee clucked. "You've heard of fetal-alcohol syndrome? Most unfortunate thing!"

I passed a hand over my eyes, and when I withdrew it the pathetic vision was mercifully gone.

Coffee was saying: "Unfair, of course, to blame it on me. Such children are born every day. The thing is, they require souls like anybody else, and that *is* my department. In this case, now: What could I do for the child more helpful than to lend it the strongest soul I know, one that will be equal to the struggle it faces in life?"

Carried away on the stream of his mocking unctuousness, Coffee had relaxed his guard, the lightning bolt guttering to a mere spark in his broadly gesturing hand. In a moment I had seized the spear from the post and fallen on him with it!

It passed through his body with a gratifying crunching sound. I held him on the spear like a pig on a spit, my face pressed grinning against his own. The look of wonder and surprise I beheld there! He drew in his breath with a great rush and with such force that it set my hair to streaming in his face. The sound was like that of a gale in winter boughs.

Then Coffee darkened with rage and, to my horror, began to rise! Feeling no tug on the spear, I looked down and saw him moving through it as freely as if he were vapor. There was no sign of a wound. The sound I had heard as the spear went in and that I had taken for the crushing of flesh and bone? I had disemboweled the chair!

Coffee had the advantage of me there, for the invulnerability did not go both ways. The next thing I knew I was lying on the floor, wracked with pain, lightning crackling around my head. I could smell my hair burning.

Coffee grimly intoned my sentence.

"I could send you on your way like Lewis and Floyd, but at present you are more useful to me up here — as a horrible example! Tell all the tales you want. You have no proof of anything, and anybody you might convince in spite of that will see that your stories do not have happy endings!

"Eventually," he said darkly, "I will find a situation for you on Earth that is commensurate with your deserts. You can entertain yourself in the meantime with speculating on what that might be.

"Use your imagination!"

CHAPTER 14

That fateful skirmish with Counts the Coffee took place in 1976. For nearly forty more years Coffee kept me in the HHG to twist in the wind — or do I flatter myself? I now think it just as likely he simply misplaced me in his mind.

I'm afraid I did nothing during this period to call myself to his attention. The problem was not fear but lack of an effective platform and, I suppose, simple demoralization. Years of contending against Coffee in two worlds, with so little to show, had blunted my spear. I looked on with a feeling of inevitability as he maintained his sway in the HHG and affairs on Earth went, with one interruption, from bad to worse.

The shining exception was the Reagan-Bush years, 1981-1992. Ronald Reagan, who finally captured the White House in 1980, was that rarest of presidents, one who arrived with a plan other than perpetuation of himself in office for eight years.

Talk about a leader holding up a vision of the good and true! "You can do it!" he told Americans, rallying them from their Stagflation Blues to an unprecedented run of prosperity.

His boldest plan was to abandon "détente" with the Soviet Union — that policy by which we had been getting skunked around the world. Reagan called the Evil Empire by its right name and took the fight to the communists. With an arms buildup at home and missiles in Western Europe; with support for anti-communist fighters in Central America and Afghanistan; with the Strategic Defense Initiative — he made things so hot for the Soviets that they finally melted down.

All these measures had to be wrung from a Congress still shaken in its nerve by the failed Vietnam war (when not actively hostile to the notion of victory over the Soviet Union). To do it, Reagan called on the help of the American people, who responded with a flood of support their representatives could not ignore.

Leadership, again.

The results speak for themselves in the fall of the Soviet Union without a shot; in the greatest liberation of human beings — the Iron Curtain millions — in the history of the world; and in dissipation of a forty-year threat of nuclear war.

Revisionists will stand on their heads trying to assign other causes or award credit elsewhere. I am confident history will affirm that Ronald Reagan — that sunny man — made all the difference.

This interval must have had Counts the Coffee scrambling to play catch-up. But not without effect, as the American electorate lost its concentration soon enough, returning to business as usual with election of that pants-dropping chucklehead, Bill Clinton. Within weeks we had the astonishing spectacle of Washington waging war against its own citizens in Waco, Texas, finally sending seventy-six of them — men, women and children — up in smoke.

This was an appropriate introduction to two decades of decline and danger, including a breathtaking plunge to the edge of insolvency.

Then, one dreary day in March, I was walking down the street, bent into the wind, when I met someone coming the other way in a motorized wheelchair. He was all bundled up, and I never would have known him if we hadn't gotten hung up in one of those awkward, excuse-me exercises.

"I beg your pardon," I mumbled, stepping to meet him on the right.

"So sorry," he muttered, wheeling and following me the other way.

Our eyes met, and I recognized Counts the Coffee! We finally got free of one another, and I plunged on my way, heart pounding. I had seen no point in speaking. Evidently he felt the same, for I was spared the jocular thrust I was braced for. Or — deflating thought — had I receded to such a small footnote in his history that he didn't know me any longer?

Not to worry — Coffee had not achieved his prominence by forgetting old scores. Hazarding a look back, I saw him sitting where I had left him, but turned in his chair to stare after me.

That very night, in my sleep, I was whisked to that obscure lying-in stall in a barn in North Dakota, where our story began. We are now up to date.

CHAPTER 15

I made the river bottom at Fort Clark my home for nearly a year. This was an extensive woodsy pasture occupied by a tribe of my own — Black Angus. The residents adopted me as a poor lost lamb, offering me not only sustenance but protective coloration!

To be sure, my lack of an ear tag and brand still would have given me away to a close observer. But we saw little of our owner in the summertime; and there was plenty of room, when his pickup did come prowling around, for me to keep out of the way.

I had no regular mama, the good lactating ladies deciding in council to pass me around, so I should be a drain on no one of them. So, I made out very well, yet was spared the necessity of cultivating in my heart, which still belonged to Mother, room for somebody else. Milk itself soon became secondary, as I turned increasingly to grass.

Life on that big semi-wild bottom was a liberation after the dull highland pasture at the Dolans'. Here I enjoyed the run of a tract as various as it was lush. There were American elms, cottonwoods and ash, and sweet meadows beside the river. Our neighbors were the deer and wild turkey. I dined again, in seasonal succession, on the Juneberries, chokecherries and bullberries I had enjoyed as a man so many years ago.

Over this expanse we cattle wandered as we pleased and were wonderfully self-sufficient. In the matter of water, for instance, there was no lining up for a turn at the tank, with its cowflop and flies; we drank where and when we pleased, in the river or in the Clark Creek slough. A lot of little freedoms such as this encouraged a spirit of independence even in the steers. A rancher would have called us half-wild, like our home.

Led by me, the calves took to swimming in the river on hot days; the heat that at the Dolans' would have been an occasion for mute suffering was diverted to sport.

Another comfort: I resorted to my old town as often as I liked, via the path leading up from the old boat landing.

This would be at night, preferably by the light of the moon, when ancient ghosts hovered on the margin of visibility. Occasionally a coal train would clank past to break the spell, and the power plants — regular Christmas trees of light — kept up a constant hum. But it was easy to make peace with these modest intrusions; they beat having to look over your shoulder all the time for the Sioux!

In July, a bull was turned in with us and kept things stirred up for six weeks. He was about as courtly as old Buster, and it occurred to me that a fellow with half a line of pillow talk could have taken those women away from him in a minute. Of course, he'd have had to whip the big guy first, and I was too little to think of jumping him or his cows. (Although this year's heifer crop was beginning to look good.)

After the bull was excused, we settled into a langorous run of shortening summer days — season of tasseling corn, ripening small grains and the choral tick and buzz of insects. The merger with fall was without a seam — fall, however, the surviving partner, the lengthening nights sharpening toward frost.

I recalled the feeder market, and was ready to bolt for the woods at the first sign of trouble. But the roundup, when it came, was of yearlings only, and I was able to relax my guard for a while.

Before the onset of winter, I made the transition to an all-grass diet. When the snow began to fly, the grass was supplemented with hay. This was dispensed by our owner on twice-daily visits, when my fellows forgot their wildness so far as to throng out to meet the tractor.

I dared not join them in this; and, if the owner lingered, the food might be nearly gone before I got there. Finally, I had to browbeat a few of the steer calves into hanging back with me until the coast was clear. I disliked throwing my weight around in this manner, but was impressed at how they submitted without a murmur. A bull, I was learning, had his prerogatives.

This was brought home even more forcibly the following spring. It was on one of our first really hot days, a dreaming May afternoon of magical properties. The birds were as noisily celebrative as usual, but otherwise an enchanted stillness prevailed, unruffled by so much as a breeze. Spring had descended on the trees in a gauzy green mist, and the light was milkily radiant.

There was in the air — how shall I describe it? — a sappy *something* that had me feeling queer all day.

I was strolling along the river, puzzled and somewhat bothered, trying to figure out what this something was. The water slid past, smooth and uncommunicative. I needed a sign, something by which to bring this pastoral dazzle into focus, into some sort of relation to myself.

The trail I was following dipped into a jungle of chokecherry trees and emerged onto a beach. Coming out the far side, I was stopped in my tracks by a novel sight. Not fifty feet away, on a blanket in the sandy shade of a black willow, were a boy and girl in romantic dishabille.

I recognized neither them nor their vehicle, a pickup; these were trespassers, nobody from whom I needed to hide. Still, to withdraw would have been the gentlemanly thing; for, although a cooler and picnic hamper lay nearby, clearly I was too late, or too early, for lunch.

But I was not thinking like a gentleman. I was not really thinking at all, except to note with some resentment that here was yet another of those sensual distractions that had had me on the trot all day to no purpose. Anyway, entranced or maybe just stubborn, I held my ground.

Then the girl saw me — and what a scramble! Grabbing up their clothing, the two of them retreated to the other side of the tree, through the feathery switches of which I saw them trying to dress while peering out at me fearfully.

I was puzzled at this behavior, not understanding why they should mind me any more than they did the birds. Also, I regretted having interrupted their fun. By way of apology, and to show friendliness, I advanced on the willow, doing my best to wag my tail.

This did not have the desired effect. The girl squealing, they stumbled and hopped, half-dressed, to the pickup and climbed inside. Alarmed at how I had alarmed them, I pursued no further. I was ready to go on my way, when I heard this from the girl:

"We can't go yet. The ugly brute has got our things."

She must have meant the hamper and cooler. I did not much care for that 'ugly brute,' especially coming from one whose own charms were, by my old human yardstick, marginal at best! When the boy then began leaning on the horn, I'm afraid it awoke the mischief in me. I approached them on the driver's side, at which the window was hastily rolled up.

"What else did you get for your birthday?" I kidded.

This came out rather louder than I intended, and seemed to startle the honker. He and his girlfriend exchanged looks positively pale.

"The hell with the things," I heard him say, through the glass. "We're getting out of here."

I stepped back and allowed them to spin away through the sand and into the trees. I listened to their diminishing roar until the white heat and birdsong had healed around it again, leaving me, if anything, more dissatisfied than before.

For consolation I turned to my captured booty. Lunch — or most of it — had been consumed. I did find in the hamper half a sack of nacho chips, which I polished off, and a twin pack of Hostess cupcakes (very good). There was a box of condoms — enough for several picnics — and what turned out to be the real prize, a battery-powered radio.

In the cooler, I would have settled for a pop. Imagine my gratified surprise when I discovered, on ice, a half-dozen cans of beer!

I had developed a taste for the stuff in the HHG. An hour or so and six cans later, I found myself standing in the shallows of the river, giving my most profound attention to my reflection in the water. It showed me what I never should have learned otherwise, that at age one I was already as tall as a full-grown two-year-old, even if I did have some filling out to do. No wonder the young couple had been frightened!

I frightened myself — but not so badly that I could bear, for the longest time, to tear myself away. My head buzzed pleasantly, and the hormones set up a regular dancing in my blood. Another image began to tease at me — that of the girl as she had stooped to retrieve her bloomers — and I bounced a mighty bellow off the bluffs on the other side of the river. It sounded so impressive I tried a second one, and then another. What a set of pipes!

I don't know where, left to myself, I would have gone with this. As it happened, I was saved from anti-climax by the timely appearance, down the same chokecherry trail I have described, of a glossy heifer of the herd.

Had she been attracted by my basso blasts? It is probable; although, having established herself in plain sight on the beach, she affected not to notice me, turning her back to crop at the few poor spears of grass growing there.

Oh, she was a real coquette! I watched her sway from blade to blade with little dance steps, tail switching across her silken flanks, and a red mist descended on my sight. Inside my head, however, everything was coming clear. The two-legged girl had put me on the right scent but tricked me into thinking like a man. Here, before my eyes, was the real solution to my day-long restlessness!

With a snuffling sob of recognition, I made for her, splashing noisily through the shallows. The little dear continued to act quite oblivious. Only when I was close enough to smell the sun on her heat-absorbent blackness did she look up — and then of course it was too late for even a good girl to make her escape!

CHAPTER 16

Thus did I enter into my sensualist phase, a brief-enough fling — with, however, consequences for others I should have foreseen and that I truly regret.

In the weeks that followed, I made the beast with six legs with all the girls, never dreaming I deserved anyone's censure. I learned everybody's name; and, with the exception of that first time on the beach, always asked before coupling up, a courtesy I think the girls appreciated.

Another new diversion was my captured radio. It wasn't *The Bismarck Tribune*, but it did put me back in touch with the world. I was delighted to be able to listen again to the indispensable Rush Limbaugh. (Although, to conserve my precious batteries, I restricted myself to one hour of Rush a day.) I also stumbled upon my old newspaper friend, Ed Advancing Along, who turned out to be a multi-media threat.

Nothing the white man did to American Indians in the days of armed conflict — not Sand Creek, not Wounded Knee — equals the cruelty of the reservation system he imposed on them.

This is the cruelty that has kept on giving, generation after generation, down to the present day. It consists of encouraging dependency in place, of making economic cripples of able-bodied men and women.

To be sure, there are Indians — typically, farmers and ranchers — who have legitimate business on the reservation. Nearly everybody else needs to get out — including most of the cops and social workers, who would not be needed in the first place except for the pathologies attendant on the reservation system.

Reservations might have been justified as an interim strategy, while Indians took the necessary step — as the conquered everywhere have had to do throughout history — of learning the ways of their conquerors. But did anybody imagine, back then, that reservations would still be around after 125, 150 years?

Ask yourselves where American blacks would be today, if the freed slaves had been settled on reservations.

At the heart of the problem is the mistaken name of 'nation' applied by European-minded white men to every least Indian tribe.

You could as reasonably confer nationhood on the Pennsylvania Dutch — or on North Dakota's Germans from Russia. The name suggests something rather more grand than the typical Indian tribe, whose numbers would make an unimportant small town — with the economic opportunities to match.

As they love themselves and their children, most Indians should do as people from the small towns have been doing for seventy-five years or more — get out! Get out and save themselves before it's too late.

They don't have to give up their identity as Indians or their rights, such as they are, in the tribe and reservation.

But they have rights in the whole country, like all Americans, not just in the reservation. They should give themselves the full use and enjoyment of them.

Speaking of full use and enjoyment: I'm afraid that after a time I made myself altogether too much at home at Fort Clark, becoming careless in the matter of concealment.

One evening I was discovered right out in the open, *in flagrante*, by my unknowing host, the rancher.

He roared down on us in his pickup. My first impulse — so bold had I become — was to resent the interruption. I uncoupled, my heifer clattered away, and I stood glowering and pawing the ground. The truck lurched to a halt a few yards away. The driver, a short fat man, did not try to get out, but just sat there looking at me, face suffused with rage and disbelief.

"Just try something, I dare you," I rumbled. In truth, I was taken aback. The man's passion had got my brain to working.

A minute later he took off the way he had come, practically airborne. I knew I would see him again soon, probably with reinforcements.

With no time to waste, I headed for the woods at a high lope. My bravado had quite collapsed, letting in sickening regret. In my carelessness I had forfeited my hideaway and playground. I was numb, in a state of shock.

Nor was that all. The rancher's anger had opened my eyes to my real offense. I had doubtless impregnated many of his cows — not only prematurely, which meant that calving would start in the difficult dead of winter, but with a maverick seed foreign to his registered line. Little wonder he had been beside himself!

So it was with no very light heart that I retrieved my few poor things from a hollow tree and packed them in the picnic hamper. There was my radio, plus some pottery fragments and trade beads I had taken from the town as keepsakes.

The sunlight lay at a red slant on the bottoms as I emerged from the woods with the hamper in my mouth and made for the river. My idea was to cross to the woods on the other shore and hole up there for the night to think over my situation.

I had just waded into the water, floating the hamper before me, when I heard the trucks coming. By the time they drew up on the bank, I was swimming. I heard the voices of men in hasty consultation — and then the water began spitting angrily all around me.

The wicked-sounding reports told the tale — they were shooting at me, for heaven's sake!

CHAPTER 17

Again, I had failed to put myself in the rancher's place. To him, I was a public nuisance that, moreover, did not enjoy the protection of being anybody's property. (No brand.) I was lucky he hadn't had a gun with him the first time.

I made the other bank safely, however, and melted into the woods. The men had no way of following; the nearest bridge, at Washburn, was fifteen miles away, and darkness near at hand. Tomorrow, however, would be a different story, and I surmised I had better put on some miles between now and then. I waited for full dark, then struck out up the river.

The *Tribune* had a wry story (which caught up with me months later) about the mysterious picnicking bull and the hunt he set off. The day after my narrow escape, two parties of armed men descended on the east bank — one above and one below my crossing place — and began walking toward each other. The sweep, or squeeze, was on.

I watched the upper party pass from the safety of a wooded island. My presence there, out of the way, was a matter of pure luck, for I had not anticipated such a thorough search. I had swum over first thing in the morning, attracted by a mysterious and persistent clanking of bells. It turned out the island was full of sheep.

I knew the race only by reputation. For their part, they thought me the most curious thing they had ever seen. I had enough of the animal in me not to resent, and even to participate in, the various sniffing measurements by which the four-legged fraternity gets acquainted. (Amusing to speculate whether early humans might have introduced themselves in the same way.)

However, there was only one of me, whereas they must have numbered twenty-five or thirty. As their guest, I was obliged to take an interest in them all; although I will say that, after a while, one sheep smells very like another.

The newspaper told how the hunting parties met, several

miles downriver, in a great confusion of the wildlife each had driven before it. The hunt then adjourned to the Hiway Bar in Washburn, where the reporter caught up with it.

By now, my status had become semi-mythical. "It's as if he grew wings and flew away," allowed one participant. Giving the headline writer back in Bismarck all the prompting he needed for *Bull flies in Washburn?*

I hung around Sheep Island for several days, letting my notoriety die down. I could have stayed longer, for my hosts were as gracious as could be. But I didn't speak the language, which made for rather long days. And I was afraid of giving their owner a chance to show up and ignite the excitement all over again. Anyway, by now I had my plan of action.

From its Missouri mouth, at Stanton, the Knife River meanders west for a hundred miles, through country increasingly remote, to its source at the divide of the *Little* Missouri River. There one can pick up one of the creeks that drops you into the heart of the *Mauvaises Terres*, or Badlands, so named for their difficulty of navigation rather than inhospitality.

In fact, their lush grasses, and the protection offered by the broken terrain, have made them a favored pasturing ground from time immemorial. In the old days, we found buffalo in abundance in the *Mauvaises Terres*. Later, Teddy Roosevelt was among the white men who ran cattle there; they are home to more than four hundred ranches to this day.

Here, if anywhere, I could lose myself amid congenial company and live out my days free from harrassment.

The sickle of a new moon hung in the west on the night I set out, swimming over to the Stanton shore.

It was tough going early on. There was the floundering around in the dark, daylight travel being out of the question. (Although the waxing moon lent me assistance night by night.) The shortness of the nights, at the approach of the solstice, didn't help. I had barely begun a night's march, it seemed, when the brightness of the sky over my shoulder required me to find cover for another too-long day.

Then there were the fences, which I could not just pop through as I had as a youngster. At first I either looked for a gate or, more often, resorted to the tricky riverbed itself. Then I wised up and began addressing fences with a wire cutter — my teeth!

I learned not to be a slave to the river in its endless divagations, but to short-cut these as visibility allowed and showed me the way. I abandoned my picnic hamper, to the relief of my aching jaws; the radio — even Rush, if you can imagine — had subsided to a whisper, anyway.

After I had put Hazen and Beulah behind me, there were no more towns, and I made easier progress. The farms were larger, the houses and fences further apart. By the light of the moon, the broad valley of the Knife presented one half-remembered scene after another. I relaxed some, deciding I was looking at a long life in the Badlands and there was not such a rush to get there. One time I found some cows handy to the river and a good concealing grove, and actually laid over for a couple of days.

The ladies were generosity itself, and a good time was had by all. However, I had acquired a conscience in these matters, and practiced early withdrawal to frustrate the sacred aim of nature. (An old Mandan practice and our most effective means of population control, after the Sioux.)

There were other diversions, such as chasing coyotes, by which I varied the routine. Still, by the time the last-quarter moon came around, I must have been at least halfway to my Badlands goal. That same night, my journey was sabotaged — the culprit being the usual suspect, myself.

It happened this way:

I was crossing state Highway 8, north of the village of Marshall. There on the west shoulder of the road, where fate had arranged I couldn't miss it, was a case of beer.

It must have fallen from the back of somebody's truck. The carton had burst, and a good many of the cans were spoiled. Not to be deterred, I dragged the wreckage to the ditch for examination. Wouldn't you know, there must have been nine

71

or ten unbroken cans, their contents mostly settled down after their rough landing. I was feeling entitled, after my three-week travels, and tested their goodness one after another.

Their goodness was … good! I stayed with them to the last drop — which, consumed, and after casting about to make absolutely sure there were no more, I returned to the trail.

Proceeding, I tried out my voice on some old corn songs and on an Ernest Tubb number or two. Then I seemed to pick up choral accompaniment. At first I thought it was only an acoustical freak, an echo. Then I realized I didn't even have to open my mouth to produce it. I had company!

Here is where things get fuzzy. I retain a picture of multiple corrals beside the river in the moonlight. The first ones held horses, steers and calves; but my singers were not there. I found these in the last corral — an incredibly various assortment of bulls. They were of several common farm breeds but also included an exotic — a Texas longhorn! There must have been twenty head in all.

I could not imagine the purpose for which such a motley group had been assembled. It could not have been for music, for the racket they made was as unmelodious as it was incessant. I had them in a regular uproar.

The longhorn was particularly bellicose, and harped on the misfortune that would be mine if it weren't for the fence that separated us.

"But, my friend — that's an impediment that is easily solved."

So saying, I opened the gate with my mouth and walked in. The effect on the company was dramatic, their din swallowed that fast in an uncanny hush. You could hear a nervous shuffling of feet and nothing else.

At last the longhorn cleared his throat and spoke up. "Say, what's the name of that last song you were singing, anyway?"

They turned out to be a regular bunch of fellows, and none better than their ringleader, and my erstwhile challenger, Longhorn Sam.

I can't begin to recall all we talked about — the outrageous lies we told, the wonderful jokes. (Young bull to old bull, spying a bevy of bovine beauties: "Father, what do you say we run up that hill and make love to a couple of those ladies?" Old bull: "Nay, my son. Let us walk up the hill and make love to them all.")

This was my first adult association with other bulls, an experience as intoxicating as the beer I had enjoyed. My companions had intelligence, imagination and wit — qualities not usually associated with the bovine race. Here were cattle as they were meant to be — a far cry from the unmanned, artificial creatures of popular imagination. They made me proud to be a bull.

Alas, a curtain of oblivion falls all too early on my memory of the most sociable night of my life to date. Sam assured me later that I was a hoot to the very end. In the middle of a group singalong on "Waltz across Texas," my legs simply folded under me, and I was asleep before the rest of me touched the ground.

When the curtain rose again, daylight was sticking painful fingers in my eyes, and everything was in motion around me. I could hardly breathe for the dust and commotion of dense bodies overhead. I was kicked in the ribs. "Get up! Get up!" somebody mooed impatiently.

I struggled to my feet and tried to keep them as I absorbed body checks on every side. Then I was actually lifted off them and borne forward on a tide of cattle!

Sick, the cogs of my mind whirling but catching nowhere, I tried to think of where I was and how I had got there. Next, I saw men hanging from a gate, directing traffic. Ahead was a loading chute, up which my fellows were herding with scarcely a murmur into the back of a long stock trailer.

I tried to put on the brakes, but independent movement was impossible. I trumpeted a warning, at great cost to my splitting head. I did it over and over.

Beside me, a voice said: "Oh, pipe down. What in the world are you bellowing about?"

His long horns flashed in the sun, and I thought his face looked familiar. He heard out my breathless explanation, then laughed in rude derision.

"Slaughterhouse, my ass — whatever that is. I told you all about it last night, don't you remember? We're only going to the rodeo."

CHAPTER 18

"It's not a bad life," Longhorn Sam said, as we rolled down the highway. "I've been at it for three years, and I know the ropes."

He went on: "You work a couple of days a week, in season, and are off the rest of the year. You get to travel around some and see the country. (It sounds like you've got gypsy blood in you, anyway.) And they treat you right — the eats are strictly top-shelf.

"Of course, I expect food isn't a big selling point with you right now."

Truly, I was in the dry-heaves stage of the disease and only half-listening. My heart's distress was at least equal to my stomach's — especially when, reaching Interstate 94, we turned and headed east, away from the Badlands. I had done it properly this time: Every five minutes down the road undid, reversed, a night or two's laborious march, with the end I knew not where. I could have laid down and died.

On the curves I could see out the slats the caravan we made. There were four tractor-trailers for the animals; a flatbed truck of hay; and a pair of travel trailers, pulled by pickups, for the two-legged help.

When I was feeling some better, I asked where home was.

"Oh," Sam said, "that is at the Ranch of Junked Farm Machinery."

"Not where we were last night?"

"Oh, no. That's only where we put on our last show."

With that information went my last hope, that eventually I would be able to resume my journey at the point of interruption.

After an hour or so on the four-lane, we slowed, and there was a stir of interest. "I remember this place," said Sam.

There was a big hill that looked like a dinosaur's back and, on top, a gigantic statue of a Holstein cow. My fellow passengers were much taken with this tribute to one of our own and could not say enough about it.

When we angled onto the off ramp, I read a familiar name on the sign: New Salem. That was only twenty miles from my old Hannover neighborhood!

We unloaded, and were turned out with the other stock in a pasture adjacent to the rodeo grounds, in the shadow of the Holstein Mount Rushmore. It was a pleasant spot, with a good stand of grass. Soon everybody was cropping happily; even I was ready for a bite. Obeying my old reclusive instincts, I retreated to the furthest corner of the pasture, not realizing I had already been noticed.

"Here comes our leader," said Sam, who had accompanied me. I tried to act nonchalant, but was alert in every nerve end when the pickup, with two men inside, drew abreast and paused. The driver, a grizzled old fellow with a few days' worth of whiskers, eyed me critically. A can of beer sat in front of him on the dash.

"We loaded him this morning," his companion said. "I told you about the open gate. Think this is somebody's idea of a gag?"

"Expensive gag," the driver grunted. He considered for a minute. "Well, he belongs to us now if he belongs to anybody. Rangy critter, ain't he? Let's just run him out there in the first 'go' tomorrow and see if he's half as wild as he looks."

"Boss, you don't even know if he'll buck," the other protested.

"That makes it more interesting," the Boss said. "Fact, I got ten dollars that says —"

But they were already moving again, and the thinking of his ten dollars was lost on the air.

Sam was amazed to learn that I had understood the rest of the conversation. "But where did you learn to do that?" he asked.

"It's just something I picked up. But how about it? Do you think I'd be any good in the rodeo?"

I had been thinking fast and hard since we hit town, and decided the rodeo life looked pretty good for the present. I was tired of being a refugee. Here, with the troupe, was the opportunity for a breather — if I could make myself useful.

"I won't say there's nothing to it," Sam said. "But I can give you some pointers. For the rest of it, just keep your eyes open tomorrow. Watch me at work — I'm one of the best."

New Salem's was typical, I would learn, of the small-time rodeos that made up our circuit. There were bleacher seats, but a good part of the crowd just milled around or watched from folding chairs in the box of their pickups. It was a homey affair, with lots of dust, pretty girls, small children and rooting for the local cowboys.

Unfortunately for Sam's strategy, I was first out of the chutes in the bullriding section. I had paid close attention to the bronc riding, however, and thought I knew roughly what was expected of me. I waited nervously as the rider took his seat and unseen hands tightened the bucking strap somewhere in front of my privates. From the arena announcer I learned I had been christened 'Maverick.'

Then the gate was pulled open. The cowboy moved on my back, and I bolted for daylight.

I got a taste of the spurs right off. Sam had warned me about this feature, but it still made me mad. I lost my head, rearing and pawing the air with my forelegs. This caused me no little discomfort from the bucking strap, but the cowboy slid off my back like a sack of potatoes. I heard him go 'plop' in the soft arena dirt.

I turned around to look at him. He picked himself up, cussing and shaking his head. Then one of the clowns came after me with a broom. Sam had told me about this part of the routine too, and I knew it was my cue to go. As I trotted for the exit, herded between the pickup men, I heard laughter from the crowd. Correctly, I guessed I had done something wrong.

"Are you on drugs?" Sam wanted to know, after the show. "Bulls don't buck like that, for Pete's sake."

By now I knew this very well for myself — from watching subsequent rides — and was stung and embarrassed.

"I got rid of my man, anyway," I shot back, a jab at Sam for having failed to do so with his more orthodox approach. Indeed, it seemed to me that the better riders knew what their bulls were going to do before they did it.

Listening in on snatches of chute talk, at New Salem and elsewhere, I confirmed that there was a 'book' on most of the bucking stock. "This one's a good bucker," I heard of one bull, "but he won't turn 'til he runs into a fence."

Other moves seemed built into the genes and were usually the same, animal to animal. When a bull started to spin, for instance, he usually could be counted on to continue in the same direction, around and around, allowing his rider to lean to the inside and "look into the well" with a certain amount of confidence.

This is to take nothing away from the performance of Sam and his fellows, which was punishing and dramatic. What it needed was headwork.

Announcement of my name at the night show brought a buzz from the spectators. They wondered what I would pull this time. So did the cowboys gathered by the chute to razz the cowboy who waited somewhat nervously on my back.

"Nothing to it, George," cried one. "Just pretend you're riding a bronc."

But I had something else in mind for this time. When the gate opened, I bounded into the arena with a series of twisting, high-kicking bucks. My rider stayed with me and was rewarded with a roar from the crowd. I went into a counterclockwise spin, continuing to kick. All the while, I tried to keep the eight-second clock in my head. I felt the cowboy shift his weight, and when I figured he was nice and comfortable, I just — stopped.

He was gone, like the cork from a bottle, before I had fairly reversed myself.

When the gun went off an instant later, the people were so quiet you could hear the echo off Holstein Hill. Then their reaction of amazed delight enveloped me. They were cheering for the bull! This was heady stuff, and I staggered erect to acknowledge their tribute. (This was to become my trademark.) Then I made for the exit.

On the way, I came face to face with the Dolan boy, who was tending the gate.

He gave me a funny look; but I realized afterward that was because, in my surprise, I had paused to stare at him. My heart was beating like crazy, and I waited for him to expose me before the world.

Of course, he didn't know me at all. I snapped out of it and continued on my way.

After the show, the Boss was visiting with some of the cowboys in Lenny's Beer Garden, an open-wall tent with picnic tables and colored lights beside the pasture. I had practically a front-row seat on the conversation, which was mostly about me.

"Where'd you get him?" one kid wanted to know. "You didn't have him two weeks ago, in Carson."

The Boss wasn't giving anything away, claiming to have won me "off some feller in a card game, I disremember where."

The proprietor was a stocky, jovial fellow in a sequined western suit that might have been lifted, warm, off of Porter Wagoner. He spotted me standing on the edge of the rainbow-colored light and laughed.

"He looks like he's waiting for somebody to set him up!"

My tongue was not exactly hanging out, but he so accurately read my mind that I could not help wagging my tail and taking a couple of excited steps in place.

Everybody laughed then; and Lenny, rummaging around, came up with a dish. However, I took the beer can from his hand before he could open and pour it; I did not need to start lapping beer like an animal now.

This made such a hit, I had to pop and chug a second one, and a third. Lenny recorded the event with a flash camera. "They'll want this at the Journal," he said. He was right -- and I made the newspapers again, the wire service picking it up this time.

CHAPTER 19

In the weeks that followed, Maverick became a celebrity around tank-town North Dakota. Neither at New Salem nor anywhere else could a rider stay with me, and I began to command more newspaper ink than the two-legged performers. My coming to town was the stuff of headlines in *The Weekly Wipe*. My name and mug appeared on all the rodeo bills and flyers, above a legend of the Boss' coinage:

WEARS NO MANS BRAND
NEVER BEEN RODE

I would be lying if I said I didn't enjoy it. The people flocked out as soon as we hit town to see me and take my picture. The cowboys, drawing their rides before the go-round, speculated with good-humored morbidness on who would be "the seven-second man." What I had begun only half-heartedly and out of necessity at New Salem I was now driven by pride to keep up.

As it happened, our early travels took us nowhere near the Badlands. If they had, I doubt I would have taken the opportunity to jump ship. What for, when I no longer needed to hide? I had been legitimized by a career!

The other bulls had their noses badly out of joint, and when the Boss let his favoritism completely run away with him, even Longhorn Sam stopped talking to me.

Not that I was in danger of dying of loneliness. When the reliability of my gentle nature (outside the arena!) had been established, the crew treated me less like a bull than a large pet dog. Except on show days, I was not confined to the pasture but had the run of the camp.

If the hired hands regarded me as domesticated, to the Boss I was "almost human." The grizzled old man talked to me all the time, and had a disconcerting way of winking at me, as if he were in on my secret. Behind his back, the other men shook their heads.

He was a constant drinker, appearing in the door of his trailer mornings sleep-touseled and with a can already in hand. The drinking grew worse, if anything, as he began to be agitated by dreams of greed and glory — dreams to which I was the key.

"This time next year," he confided in his whiskery voice, "we won't be in a hunnert miles of a shithole like this here. We'll hire out to the big shows — like Mandan! Maybe we'll even get down into South Dakota and Wyoming."

He took another pull and sighed deeply. "You and me," he said, favoring me with a conspiratorial and bloodshot wink.

Let him dream as big as he pleased — it was his betting that made me nervous.

Like the drinking, this became more extravagant all the time, until he might have several thousand riding on one of my performances. He bet with the cowboys and with the public. The day before a show, he would tour the local watering holes. There he made himself so obnoxious that people were happy to put up a hundred or two in hopes of seeing the drunken old braggart put in his place.

He gave them odds and all. The bar owner held the stakes. After the show, the Boss went around to collect and buy the house a drink. This seldom failed to produce a stir that fanned betting on my next ride. He knew how to work 'em, all right.

Beer and the freedom to come and go were not my only 'fringes.'

With an eye to producing a race of Mavericks, the Boss went out and bought me my own harem — five 'open' cows. For Sam and the other bulls, this was the last straw, and they bellowed their outrage to the world whenever I was entertaining. "That's all right," the Boss chortled. "It'll make 'em meaner."

Their racket created no very tender atmosphere for romance. Neither, for that matter, did the behavior of the Boss. He liked to watch — half-shot, of course, the obligatory can in hand — and encourage me on. "Go on, knock her up!" he would cry, and laugh like a crazy man.

Then one night, way over in the eastern part of the state, in a little Red River Valley town, my streak came to an end.

I had been off my feed all day, possessed of a peculiar lassitude and lightheadedness. I tried to signal my condition to the Boss, but he took no notice. When the time came for my ride, I was weak as a kitten.

The ability to "play hurt" is the proudest boast of the true athlete, and certainly I gave it the best I had. But my body lagged behind my mind's most urgent commands, and my trademark reverse spin was a feeble parody of itself. In a daze I heard the gun go off and then the triumphant yip of my cowboy as he dropped into the clear.

Instead of cheering him, the crowd — my people — delivered themselves of a unanimous groan. Sorry for them, dismayed and ashamed, I left the arena with head bowed.

The Boss took our reversal with surprising equanimity. "I dropped twenty-six hunnert out there tonight," he admitted cheerfully, but expected to make it back — and then some — on the morrow.

"The action has been a trifle slow lately," he observed with a chuckle. "If this don't loosen up their purse strings, I miss my guess."

"But I feel terrible," I told him. So uncanny was the communication that had grown up between us, I was not surprised when he seemed to grasp my meaning exactly.

"You'll be fine tomorrow," he promised.

It happened just as he said. I awoke next day clearheaded and with a ravenous appetite. By showtime that afternoon I was bursting with energy and the ambition to avenge my loss. It did not even bother me when I saw the Boss huddling with one cowboy after another, dealing out reckless fistfuls of cash. I knew I was good for it.

As rodeo's greatest crowd pleaser, the bull riding is usually scheduled late in the show, and so it was that day. The overflow crowd was primed for it, greeting its commencement with whistles and yells. First out of the chute was Sam, who dispatched his rider in five seconds. My failure of last night had proven a real tonic for morale around the corral. "There, *that's* how it's done," Sam seemed to say, as he passed out of the arena with a haughty toss of those horns.

My cowboy was young — twenty at the outside — with a husky build and a tangle of red curls spilling from under his hat. He lounged on the top rail as I was ushered into the chute. It needed only a glance to tell he was rough and ready. He had a jut jaw and mocking, infectious grin that you took to on sight.

"Well, Mav, it's you and me for it," he twanged. "I hope you ate your Wheaties this morning."

"I'll throw you on your ass on the best day of your life," I countered.

He threw back his head and laughed, showing a mouthful of strong white teeth.

I could tell by the feel of him on my back that he was going to be a good one. Some amateurs sit too slack, and find themselves "in a storm," as they say, first jump out of the chute. Others, all tensed up, are unable to properly read their bull.

Red rested easy but not *too* easy, feeling me out, gathering information. I gave him a couple of ripples, and he touched my sides with his heels, picking out the places where the spurs would go in. I knew I could look for a good taste of the metal from this one.

"Let 'er rip!"

Red did not disappoint, raking me with punishing skill as I bounded into the clear. I started him out with some good stiff-legged jumps for his back, then tested his balance with a couple of spins around the old whirlpool. His balance was up to the job.

Figuring that, if he was any student of mine at all, he would be looking for my classical reverse, I stopped instead and "reached for the sky." This brought the usual sough of wonderment from the crowd, but Red was unimpressed.

"Never mind them," he mocked, practically in my ear. "It's *me* you've got to show something!"

Red

And spurred me on the way down, the showoff!

Truth to tell, he had just about run me out of time ~~and ideas~~. Where the *cartwheel* came from I have no idea. I had never done such a thing in any of my lives or thought of doing it. It was a mad stunt born of sheer desperation, ~~that I never would have tried if I had had more than a split second to reflect.~~ I could have crushed Red and broken a leg or two of my own in the bargain.

As it was, Red went flying in the clear, and I surprised myself by landing on all fours, even if it wasn't pretty, none the worse. My feet had scarcely touched the ground when the *gun* ~~pistol~~ went off.

The crowd was as quiet as church, ~~as if people could not believe their eyes.~~ Then a murmur arose and spread around the stands as a kind of sigh. Heart sinking, I looked around and saw Red lying on his back a dozen yards away.

Sick with remorse, I started for him. The clowns, misunderstanding, intercepted me and began flailing away with their brooms. I stood there and took it, frozen by the awful sight. In my short career, I had watched many good men limp away, but never anything this bad. Red's eyes were closed. He had lost his hat, and his face under all that dusty red hair was a ghastly white.

He looked like he was dead.

Then the ambulance crowded through the gate, red light flashing, and one of the clowns gave my tail an angry twist. For the second time in as many days I slunk out of an arena from which all joy had departed, in a silence so profound I could hear a woman remark, "Poor thing, it's not his fault."

I knew better. *from that moment my*

Later, the Boss drove out to see me. He had his winnings with him, loose, in the cab, and he showed them off by scooping up bills by the double-handful and letting them flutter around his head. He looked like a one-man tickertape parade. He laughed like a fool, and was so drunk his whiskers were full of saliva.

I turned away and started to walk off. He followed alongside in the truck, trying to wheedle me into taking a beer.

"Are you pissed because I made you take that dive?" he whined. "Promise never happen again. Come on, have little drink. Nothing in it."

So that's what had been the matter with the Old Milwaukee yesterday!

If he could have known, I was scandalized neither by the knowledge that he had drugged me nor by the certainty, despite his promise, that he would do it again, in a minute, if the "action" required it.

No. If I was through with rodeo — and I was — it was on strictly humanitarian grounds: cruelty to cowboys!

CHAPTER 20

Having made up my mind, I should have quit the rodeo game then and there, instead of hanging on and just drawing my pay, so to speak. I chose not to do so for two reasons.

First, the populous Red River Valley — farming rather than ranching country, and three hundred miles from the Badlands — was no place to cut myself loose. Then, overhearing the help, I learned our Labor Day date, only three weeks thence, was for Medora, in the very heart of the *Mauvaises Terres!*

So I would stay with the tour that long, while taking care to break no more cowboys. I would, in short, dog it (so to speak).

As we set up for our next rodeo, I tried to tip off the Boss, not wanting him to drop any money on me. Every time he came around, I growled and shook my head.

"Don't bet!" I pled with him. "Keep your money in your pocket. I'm not good for it, I tell you."

But he was too far gone in greed to put any such construction on my behavior. He thought I was only angry with him over the doping thing.

"Take it out on the cowboys," he chuckled. "I got a bundle riding on you tomorrow night."

I realized he would have to be shown.

My first rider after Red was a kid, scared to death, whose pals kept reminding him of the cowboy I had put in the hospital last week. I knew I could take no chances with this one. His knees were shaking so badly he almost knocked the wind out of me in the chute!

I responded with the prettiest waltz you ever saw. He could have had his pockets filled with eggs and never broken a one. When he jumped off after eight seconds — nearly spraining an ankle — I never saw a more relieved-looking cowboy. This was before it dawned on him that he had been had, cheated.

I never had a word of thanks from a cowboy for sparing his bones. That's because half his score depends on the ruggedness of his mount. Easy bull, automatic low score for the ride.

"Sucker didn't have no life to him at all," Fuzz Nuts snarled at the pickup man, when he had recovered his wits. He tried to spit contemptuously, but nothing came.

The Boss was furious; he had made the connection between my lackadaisical performance and my changed demeanor of late. However, he couldn't make up his mind whether I was trying to get even with him or had something the matter with me.

"If you're sick, that's one thing," he fumed. "But if I find out you're screwing the pooch, so help me God —"

"Don't bet," I lowed mournfully. "Tomorrow will be the same story."

Then I realized he had given me a better idea. Next day I stood around in a conspicuous spot with my head drooping. The Boss had the rodeo vet there in five minutes.

As the vet went over me, the Boss paced. I felt sorry for him. He didn't realize there was no suspense to it, that his dream was already dust, and there was nothing to be done for it.

"I can't find anything the matter," the vet pronounced at last. "If he doesn't snap out of it, we can always run him in for some tests. Right now, I wonder if he isn't just tuckered out."

"Tuckered out! Hee hee, that's it!"

The Boss had been so badly frightened, tiredness now appeared to him as positively desirable, a sterling quality in a bull.

"He *is* a pretty active feller, if you know what I mean," the Boss went on. "Not like you and me, hey, Doc? Hee hee!"

The vet merely grunted. He was junior to the Boss by twenty years and, unlike him, didn't look like he had been suckled on a beer bottle.

I was excused from not only the rest of the rodeo but from participation in the Boss' breeding project. "You been living too high on the hog," he announced grimly. "You're cut off 'til you show you can ride again."

He shut off the beer too. All this was very much to the satisfaction of my fellow performers, but did not make me one of the boys again. To most, I had merely added goldbricking to my list of offenses.

A surprising exception was Longhorn Sam, who approached me after we had unloaded at Glen Ullin, our last stop before Medora.

"I hope you're feeling better," he said, somewhat stiffly. (It was weeks since we had spoken.) Then, with gruff emotion: "Never mind those other guys. You're the best we have, and everybody knows it."

That gave me something to think about — that and the familiar bustle and excitement of setting up camp. No doubt about it: I was going to miss this life.

The Glen Ullin rodeo grounds are out in the country east of town, alongside the weigh station and railroad; the Twin Buttes rear whitely nearby. ('Little Maiden's Breasts,' Custer called them in his diary, enroute to the Little Big Horn.) High summer was on the land in fields of marble-green corn and nodding sunflowers. The birds had left off their singing and started thinking — their gladsome music supplanted by the husking of grasshoppers and the tick-tock of crickets.

There was a suspenseful quality to the still perfection of the days, a hint of impending departure. And I was heavy in my heart.

The Boss made it no easier for me. Our first show was Friday night; he spent a half-hour in the pasture that afternoon, bucking me (and himself) up with a kind of pleading jollity.

"We'll show 'em what-for tonight, won't we, old buddy? Yes, sir, a week of the old rest cure and we're as good as new. Ain't that right, champ?"

He beamed at me repeatedly, a grimace of desperate optimism.

So I was wavering badly when it came time for my ride, especially when I saw the Boss pacing behind the chutes, his expression a touching confusion of apprehension and hope. I was strongly tempted to suppress my squeamishness and win one for the Nipper, letting the cowboys fall where they might.

After all, whom did I owe? And the cowboys had signed up for it, hadn't they?

I was still debating the question when my cowboy eased onto my back. He seemed to sit all right, but as always there was no way to judge the brittleness of his bones.

I came pounding out with a pretty good imitation of my old disc-fusing style. This squeezed a few grunts out of him, but he stayed in good possession; so I felt safe in stepping up the pace. I signaled my first turn with my head, and he not only read that but found the leisure to give me a little rowel. Needed more of a challenge, did he? I turned then and started to take him the other way.

That's when it happened. He had overcorrected in anticipation of this now-famous maneuver and got himself loosened up. I felt him, not going, but getting ready to go.

I had him right where I wanted him — and, at the moment of crisis, I couldn't pull the trigger!

I saved his ass by straightening and high-kicking it for the fence. The gun sounded, and he stepped off as easily as from a merry-go-round. I looked around guiltily for the Boss, but he was nowhere to be seen.

Full of dread, I waited for him until long after the crowd had left and the lights gone dark. The moon rose, looking like a Mandan girl with her hair let down the left side of her face. I wandered desolately over the pasture, the chilly dew gripping my ankles. The other bulls had retired long ago. (Without a word, good or bad, for me. Sam gave me a long contemptuous look, but that was it.) I was all alone in my misery, or so I thought.

Then came a husky voice from the other side of the fence: "Lonesome, honey?"

It was Easy Susie, the most aggressively submissive of my consorts. Not really in the mood, but glad for any distraction, I snipped the barbed wire and ambled over for a visit.

I will say this for Susie: She knew how to treat company. In a little while I had so far forgotten my troubles that I never saw or heard a thing until a voice boomed, practically in my ear:

"Well, well — looky here! All recovered, are we?"

Disheveled, soaked all down one side, the Boss stood beside us shivering from the cold and with the moonlight glancing madly from his eyes. It appeared he had been sleeping on the ground and was little better for his rest. The smell of drink was on him in a cloud. He had something in his right hand with which he made a snapping sound again and again. It was a quirt.

Susie fled in terror as he fell on me and began beating me about the head and shoulders. It was the act of a madman, but of course I was not going to do him any harm. If resistance was out of the question, so — to my stubborn way of thinking — was flight. Simply, I owed the man. I lowered my head, to protect my eyes, and let him whale away.

My main concern was that he would give himself a heart attack. He thrashed me until I felt the blood trickling warm off my neck and down my nose. At last his breath came in ragged gasps, and the blows were further and further apart. Then they ceased altogether. I blinked the blood out of my eyes and hazarded a look at him in the moonlight.

The sweat poured off him, and he swayed dangerously. It took him a minute to find the wind for a parting malediction:

"I'll see you in a hot dog, you treacherous son of a bitch!"

Okay, I thought, we're even.

I washed up in a water tank, but even so my appearance at next afternoon's go-round caused a minor to-do.

"What's the matter with that animal?" demanded the arena judge, and my ride was delayed until the Boss was sent for.

Looking pale and ill, but in perfect possession of himself, the Boss explained blandly that I had cut myself on barbed wire trying to get at the cows.

The judge acted skeptical, but I was allowed to perform.

My heart had hardened somewhat toward the Boss, enabling me to cakewalk through my ride without a twinge of conscience. I may have achieved another first that day — the only performer, man or beast, to be booed in a rodeo arena. I trotted out with head held high.

The exit gate was plugged with a small stock trailer. The pickup men crowded in on either side, and I was up and in before I knew it. The Boss must have slipped them something for this extra duty. The door was slammed and bolted behind me, somebody gave a cry, and then I was moving.

The ride was not a long one — only as far as the weigh station, where dozens of cattle were being loaded onto a short string of ancient wooden stock cars on the rail siding. I surmised the Boss had seen and taken advantage of an opportunity to carry out his hot-dog threat forthwith!

I joined twenty-some steers in one of the cars. "Is this the vacation package for Las Vegas?" I inquired of the nearest head.

"They didn't say where we are going," my neighbor replied solemnly.

Soon the Boss came wheeling up. A last-minute reprieve? No — he had only come to collect his money. He was paid by a fellow waiting beside the track, and I heard him ask, "Where is he?" Our eyes found each other through the slats of my car — and the old man burst into tears!

The buyer looked at him in astonishment. As for me, I could not help the lump that rose in my throat at the ridiculous picture he made, face working in grief over an animal he had thrashed half to death only hours before.

Say what you will about him, the Boss had freedom, wore no man's brand. If there can be such a thing as a *good* asshole, that was the Boss. I looked for him to bounce back strongly with one new scheme or another; possibly as soon as Medora, the customers would feel again the prod of his priapic self-interest.

"So long, Boss," I called. "No hard feelings!"

CHAPTER 21

Toward evening our cars were picked up by a train originating in Dickinson and bound for the stockyards of South St. Paul. This was an old-fashioned livestock special, complete with an antique passenger car up front — a "drovers car" — for the owners of the animals.

My car mates did not appreciate the jostling as we were switched into the train, and really complained once we were under way and started rocking and rolling. As for me, even guessing that the end of our journey was hot dog-related, I couldn't help being excited by my first ride on the "steam cars" about which I had read in the HHG. I held to my good window vantage until the rushing air fairly dried out my eyes.

More cattle were cut in at New Salem, and then we cooled our heels while the railroad ran a hot stack train around us. It was sundown before we got our green board and trundled out of town. My fellow passengers began to complain of hunger.

"That's all right, boys — we pick up the diner at Mandan," I joked.

We never got that far. A few miles short, along a shining twilit loop of the Heart River, we "went on the ground" — derailed, piled 'em up.

Fortunately, we were just crawling, following the block of that stack train, or the damage would have been worse. We heard a racket up ahead, and then our car received a sharp wrench. Next thing, we were riding on the ties, getting the teeth shaken out of our heads. The door on the river side burst open, and a couple of steers toppled out with forlorn cries. Then our car fell on its nose, skidded some in a shower of sparks and came to rest.

We were a while untangling ourselves, and I'm afraid some at the front of the car, at the bottom of the crush, were badly hurt. Anyway, they were unable to get to their feet and struggle with the rest of us, uphill, to the open door. Others hurt themselves in the short drop to the ground. My recent athleticism on the rodeo circuit may have come to my aid here.

I landed heavily; but, regaining my feet, seemed to be intact.

Trackside, all was confusion. Up and down the train, the cattle were in full, pitiful cry — some from pain, others out of fear. As well as I could tell in the near-darkness, most of the cars were still on the rails. Those, like ours, that had jumped were still upright but missing one or more wheel sets.

More doors than ours had sprung, and dozens of cattle were soon on the ground, milling about.

I lent a hand — or, my head and shoulders — to a jammed door on a wholly grounded New Salem car, freeing the occupants.

Freeing them for what I didn't stop to consider. For myself, I recognized deliverance when I saw it. This was where the Hot Dog Express and I parted company.

I saw a pair of lanterns moving in our direction from the head end of the train — those would belong to the enginemen — and, behind those, the rosy glow of fusees, doubtless wielded by the stockmen.

I started walking back west, looking for an easy gradient down to the river. I was overtaken by a broad black shadow.

"Thank you," it said, "for helping us get out of that car back there."

I assured the New Salemite he was entirely welcome and kept moving. To my annoyance, he stuck by my side.

"Of all the people I have known," he said, "there is only one who could have done such a thing." And then, to my great astonishment, he spoke my name, Bull.

I froze, stricken, and tried to see into the darkness from which he was nearly indistinguishable.

"I am Billy," he said.

What a picture we must have made — our clumsy embraces, the joyous tears with which we watered each other! Before long, we had attracted a crowd. A private conversation was impossible under the circumstances, but I did get from Billy the one piece of information I needed.

"Your mother is fine — the same saint she always was. She has a new little boy now."

He spoke this last gently, anticipating its bittersweet impact on my heart. I didn't ask whether she still remembered or ever spoke of me. Her well-being was all I could ask for.

Billy introduced me to several of his friends from the Dolan place, none of whom remembered me. Neither did I remember them. That is, although some of the names were familiar, I could not match them with the adult shapes that pressed around us in the dark. I was not interested in them.

To my irritation, they detained us with a babble of questions and complaints.

"My leg hurts."

"When are we going home?"

"This is the last time I take the train."

"What's going to happen now?"

Billy was patient and deliberate with them; while, for their part, they obviously looked on him as a leader.

"As to that last question," he said, turning to me, "I think we can do no better than to ask this man here."

I drew Billy aside.

"The injured ones," I said, "will have to be destroyed. There is no help for it. The rest will be loaded into new cars, or trucks, and sent on their way again."

Billy nodded. "I've wondered from the first where we were going. Do you know?"

I hesitated only briefly, recalling the last time I had tried to spare his innocence.

"We were going to the slaughterhouse," I said.

"And what happens at this slaughterhouse?"

"They put a bullet in your head and cut you up into food for the Two-Legs."

He did not even blink. Later he would tell me he had always suspected something not very pretty. For him, satisfaction at having the central question of his existence cleared up — why are we here? — trumped horror or even indignation.

"And you? You will make your escape, like last time?"

I exclaimed: "Why, you and I together, Billy! Don't you see? This is our second chance at that life of adventure we used to talk about. Don't tell me you don't remember!"

"Oh, no," Billy said. "I remember very well." But he seemed to speak cautiously, rather than with the enthusiasm I had expected. The reason became apparent with his next words.

"And our friends from the farm — they can come too?"

I was stunned. I didn't consider that I had any friends from the Dolans' after Billy — not any longer, not among this dull lot. But rather than speak unkindly of them, I merely explained the impracticality of trying to run off with such a herd.

"We wouldn't get five miles," I concluded.

Billy digested this. Then: "But what do we tell them? That we propose to save ourselves and let them go to the slaughterhouse?"

"We tell them 'goodbye,'" I said impatiently. "We don't say anything about the slaughterhouse. They didn't know about the slaughterhouse before, and they don't need to know about it now."

"I know about it now," Billy said.

Just as stubborn and nimble as I remembered — the same attributes that had cost him so dearly a year ago!

"Only because I told you. But they're going to the slaughterhouse whether we leave them here or take them with us to be rounded up later. The issue is whether we go the slaughterhouse with them or get away by ourselves."

Billy's unshakable position was that, knowing what we knew, we were obliged to try to save as many of our 'friends' as we could, never mind the heightened risk to ourselves.

I'm afraid that in here I completely lost my temper. Asking Billy to remember who had gotten it right the last time, I pounded on the theme of that darkest day of his life.

"Now you propose to throw your head after your balls," I concluded savagely. "Well, mine won't be beside it."

A disgraceful performance. It turns out I had never forgiven Billy for my failure to save him that other time.

He heard me out, then turned without further comment

and started back for the others.

Of course I followed, already ashamed of myself. "Where are you going?" I blurted, knowing full well.

"Back to my friends," Billy said, his tone making it clear that I was no longer included in that category.

CHAPTER 22

I have recalled the Heart River as the hub of the Mandans in our glory days, before we were displaced by that first smallpox and the Sioux. We controlled it all the way west to its source in the remoteness of the *Mauvaises Terres* — the Badlands.

(Which is why, in the HHG, I wouldn't listen to any crying from my Sioux acquaintances when this territory was wrested from their people, in turn, by the whites.)

You can see where this is going. The Heart — beside which the train wreck had conveniently deposited me — would be my means of resuming the journey I had attempted earlier on the Knife. With the difference that now I was responsible for the secure passage of a dozen souls besides myself.

For, yes, I allowed Billy to shame me into taking on a few of his friends and a couple of others too. These would have been more numerous, I am sure, if our sales pitch had included everything. But I wanted an orderly march, not a stampede, and told Billy the whole thing was off if he said a word about the slaughterhouse.

Instead, I talked up the advantages of freedom, of calling our own shots for a change instead of having our tickets punched by the Two-Legs all the time.

The concept of freedom meant little to our audience. Some had already fallen to grazing and paid little attention; with the others, as well, food was uppermost.

Asked one: "Why should we not just settle down where we are? There is all this grass, and water is right down there."

"Your brains would make a good head cheese," I snapped, forgetting myself in my impatience to be off. "We have dallied too long already. You people must make up your minds. With you or without, Billy and I leave right now."

It was mostly without, but Billy was satisfied that everybody had had his opportunity.

If the Two-Legs observed the departure of our little party, they gave no alarm; they would not have expected us to wander far in any case. On that theory, I was satisfied that first night to simply cover ground. I cut fences recklessly and made no effort to confuse or conceal our trail.

After an hour and not more than a couple of miles, some began to complain. I asked Billy if he would drop back and make sure everybody kept moving.

His manner was still cool. "They have been through a lot," he said. "Surely it is time to call it a night."

"Listen," I said.

Our party, having slowed to a crawl, now stopped. It was possible to hear quite clearly. From east down the valley, where city lights glowed against the sky, came the crackle of rifle fire. Billy bowed his head.

"Now, let's go," I said.

I would put our night's march at five or six miles. Finally, a couple of hours before daylight, we came to a good stand of trees at a bow in the river; here was camp.

"Eat and drink your fill," I told our troops. "But don't wander far, or fail to be back here when it starts to get light."

I told Billy, "No doubt we will have to round them up when the time comes."

More tired than hungry, I flopped down under a great rustling cottonwood, and Billy joined me. The sounds of cropping and chewing came from out of the darkness around us.

"I thank you," Billy said formally, "for taking us on."

I said: "You can thank me by forgetting those hateful things I said back there. I was angry, and didn't mean them."

"You were provoked. I was asking a lot."

We were longer than that in getting back on the old comfortable terms of our Hannover days, but it was a start.

I outlined for Billy my plan of a home in the Badlands, even as I wondered privately how it could be stretched to accommodate our new numbers. He approved of the destination, but was concerned about the length of the journey.

"Over so many miles, you can't drive our people as hard as you did tonight."

I tried to impress on him that this was a race. "Anyway, it's not as if they are still being fattened for the market. These are mostly your people, and I'm counting on you to keep them motivated."

"Yet we're not allowed to mention the slaughterhouse."

"Absolutely not. Emphasize the positive. Talk to them about being free and their own boss."

I wanted to make soldiers, Mandan style, to maintain discipline on the trail. I told Billy I knew I could count on him. He suggested two others who possessed the necessary reliability and force of character. You will meet them later: solid and literal Wilbur, and Ralph, the jokester.

Even as we discussed the matter, we were about to add a fourth.

"Somebody is coming," Billy said, and even by starlight I could see him, a great white bull plodding determinedly down the trail toward our camp.

"I remember him from the train," I said, "but he didn't leave with us. I wonder what changed his mind."

He approached one of our steers and demanded, in a very loud voice, to learn the whereabouts of "your leader."

"The one with the big mouth," he elaborated.

The steer, confused before, now turned unhesitatingly in my direction, causing Billy to laugh. We rose to meet our visitor, who was no less plainspoken with us.

"See here," he rumbled, thrusting his head in my face. "My name is Duke. I've been giving it some thought, and I want to know what you meant back there by that 'head cheese' business."

Truly, this was a night for reunions!

Duke readily recalled our previous meeting, chuckling to picture me as I was then — "coyote bait, a walking midnight snack," too inconsiderable to qualify as a regular meal.

"But I see you took my advice, and now you can go where you please — at night or any other time!"

"Yes — and you took mine, which pleases me no end," I said.

"Um, yes," the Duker growled. He accepted our invitation to "take a load off," sinking to the ground — somewhat stiffly, I observed — with a groan of pleasure.

"I had to give it some thought," he said. "I'm supposed to be going back East, you know. On special assignment, you might say. They're getting up a big new breeding program back there, and wanted me to help them get it off the ground. Very prestigious, harrumph."

In the presence of a great bullslinger — when a real master is playing — I am usually all ears, a humble and respectful student. And I would have been the same way this time, if I hadn't glanced over at Billy and seen his incredulous look. Then I couldn't help myself, and burst out laughing.

Duke, deeply offended, huffed and puffed, rumbled and grumbled, and made as if to get to his feet. Suddenly an aged look stole across his face, and he settled back down with a sigh.

"The truth," he said in disgust, "is that I'm getting old. Can't split it for them like I used to! I knew I was washed up when even Bertha — remember her, boy? — went and got herself a boyfriend.

"So they shipped me out! I didn't know where to, but — no offense — I didn't much like the looks of the company I was in.

"Where were we supposed to be going, do you know? I figured it probably wasn't anyplace I'd have signed up for, myself!"

CHAPTER 23

We hid out in the woods all next day and got rested up. I had Billy take me around for introductions, starting with our prospective soldiers.

His friend Ralph accepted cheerfully enough, but seemed most interested in trying out one of his riddles on us.

Q: Why is the grass always greener on the other side of the fence?

A: Because everybody has been tramping around and going to the bathroom on this side.

"He makes them up himself," Billy admitted, as we moved on. "But don't be put off. He is sharp as a tack and absolutely reliable."

Wilbur, by contrast, was grave to the point of mournfulness. "I will do it," he tolled, of soldiering, solemn as an iron bell.

"You can bet he will, too," said Billy.

To everybody, one on one, I explained where we were going and what it would take to get there: orderly and swift movement by night, strict concealment by day, obedience to the soldiers and to me.

Fed, watered and rested, all seemed happy to agree. But, then, acquiescence was a habit with them, not a discipline. Would they be able to hold onto the thought over many wearying nights?

Everything, including the weather, went our way at first. We made good progress the next two nights, until I no longer worried about pursuit from Mandan. The danger was discovery by landowners along the route. I became particular about fences, especially those alongside a road. With these, I would cut only the bottom couple of wires and make everybody crawl through. With luck, the pattern of our vandalism would not be discovered for a while.

On the trail and in camp, over many long conversations, Billy and I got "caught up."

Billy was endlessly curious about everything that had happened to me. In this I tried to satisfy him, while omitting everything that cast a backward shadow on my previous life or on the HHG. Enough separated us at it was; and I was only too aware that he was trying, through his tireless inquiries, to determine the full extent of his losses.

For this reason, I tried to skirt or downplay certain sensitive areas, a tactic he would not allow.

"Of course you have enjoyed many women," Billy said.

"A few, of course," I admitted.

He sighed. "There are times," he said, "when I am almost up to it. I will wake in the morning all fresh, with my mind wiped clean, and the feeling strong in me. Then, before I can do anything, I remember what happened, and it's no good."

This was hard to listen to. Again, after he had heard with absorption and seeming enjoyment the story of my rodeo days, he burst out with a passion:

"If only I hadn't been such a coward! If only I had gone with you as you asked! How different everything would be today!"

How I yearned to tell him of the advantage in knowledge I had enjoyed and that accounted for our different fates! As it was, I could only try to get him to stop flagellating his adult self with his childish failure.

Of Billy's own life there was not much to tell.

"I was a real mess there for a while," he said. "I quit eating — didn't care if I lived or died. A couple of days of that and I was too weak to move. Mother gave up on me in disgust — told everybody I was going to die.

"It might have happened, too. The Dolans were otherwise occupied — looking for the one that got away! It bothered them no end, losing you like that, and they went out two or three times, trying to find you. They were sure you were hanging around somewhere close. I thought I knew better, and rejoiced — bad off as I was — when they kept coming up empty.

"'The coyotes have got him' — that's what our people said. Well, I didn't believe it, and told your mother so when she came around to check on me. She also had faith in you, but was glad to hear it from somebody else."

Billy smiled.

"It was your mother who pulled me through. No disrespect, but she has such funny ways, it's hard to stay down in the dumps when she's around. Before I knew it, I was letting her nurse me. Then, a little at a time, I began to come around."

With some friends, he revived our old expeditions. This spring, with more size going for them, they undertook what Billy called "coyote patrols." Nobody had told the coyotes about calves that behaved like that! Before long, Billy's boys had spoiled their fun by running all the coyotes out of the neighborhood!

However, with passing time Billy's playmates proved harder to coax into any kind of sport, and his pleasures became quieter and more solitary.

He took long walks, he became a student of the weather. He discovered the solace of food, of eating as an end in itself. Most of all, he thought.

Knowing nothing of feedlot or slaughterhouse, but remembering the cutting knife, he realized there had to be more to such a becalmed, stupid existence than met the eye — a kicker hidden in there somewhere. Watchful, but without fear — "The worst had already happened, right?" — he waited for the other shoe to drop.

"However, in my wildest imaginings, I never dreamed it would be you," he laughed.

* * *

Preoccupied with avoiding men, I had not considered the problem of other cattle.

We were closing in on Big Muddy Creek, on our fourth night out. I had sent the party on its way while I lingered to do some cosmetic housekeeping on a cut fence. Catching up sooner than expected, I was angered to find everyone standing around in happy, gabby consultation with about an equal number of Herefords.

Ralph was explaining to one, "Because everybody has been walking around and going to the bathroom on this side."

"I don't get it," the Hereford said.

I found Billy engaged in a conversation of his own. "What is this?" I demanded.

He acted surprised. "Why, these people live here," he said.

"I figured that out for myself. I mean, what are you doing, standing around talking when you're supposed to be marching?"

Coolly, Bill said, "I don't recall a rule against visiting with our own kind."

Of course, there was no such rule, although I now realized there should have been. I had a sudden sinking feeling.

"What have you been telling them?" I asked.

Billy disdained to answer, and my question just hung there until, finally, his new friend cleared his throat and spoke up, neither loudly nor hopefully:

"Freedom. Badlands."

Then and there Billy and I had an awful row. Billy's position was that, having dangled the Badlands — however foolishly — we were obliged to share them with the Herefords. Mine was that more people yet would surely sink the enterprise, making us impossible of concealment in the Badlands even if we survived the trail.

I threatened to abandon our original outfit if Billy did not move it out on the instant, and no Herefords to it.

The Herefords just stood about and chewed on such thoughts as they had. I was furious with Billy for forcing discussion of their case in front of them.

I got my way — but we made no very happy party crossing Big Muddy Creek. Some of our people were still nervous about getting their legs wet above the ankles, and I could not restrain myself from giving them a good tonguelashing. The mood was not just subdued but sullen. Billy fell in with the rear of the procession, abandoning the point position he usually shared with me.

It was not long before Wilbur came forward to report that the Herefords were following us.

Wearily, I put Ralph up front and, with Wilbur, dropped out of line. We could see the Herefords, dimly, by the light of the last-quarter moon, patiently pacing us at a distance of half a mile.

Do you know the bovine's rolling walk, the thrusting pump-like motion of his head? It is always the same in its artlessness, and never fails to touch my heart. A bovine does not know how to sneak or skulk.

The last of our people passed, and the Herefords kept coming until they noticed Wilbur and me. Then, fifty yards away, they stopped. They studied us but did not consult with each other, their attitude suggesting neither fear nor belligerence but simple acknowledgment that the way was blocked.

I relented.

"Go and tell them they are welcome," I told Wilbur. "I'll have our people stop until they can catch up."

Later, when we were talking again, Billy would congratulate me on having done the right thing — to which I replied, somewhat grimly, that I had done "the only thing."

Billy nodded enthusiastically and said: "Yes! If you have freedom only for yourself, you are just an outlaw, nothing more." He was becoming a regular political philosopher.

I allowed this high-minded interpretation, but in fact my turnaround had a more practical origin. There was simply no way, short of violence, that I could have kept the Herefords from following us. Soon our march must take them off their own property, when they would become strays like ourselves and, unsupervised, a threat to our security.

That's all I meant about having done "the only thing."

CHAPTER 24

There was a comical sidelight to the Hereford business. We were a more various group than before, having added cows and calves. A yearling maid by the name of Millicent, touched by his eloquence in their behalf at Big Muddy Creek, fell in love with Billy. Despite every discouragement, she followed him everywhere, and he took a lot of kidding about it, some of it rough.

"She wants something, but doesn't know what it is yet," Duke told him. "How long are you going to hold out on her, anyway?"

Billy, ruffled in his customary poise, only mumbled.

"You could at least explain the principle to her," Duke persisted, "then send her around to me for a demonstration."

I got next to Duke and put an end to that stuff, but Milly was not so easily disposed of. Her adoring persecution — never a word said, only the pad of her feet always behind him, the love-struck glaze in her big brown eyes whenever he turned around — got on Billy's nerves.

"I have important work to do, and you are always underfoot," he told her. "I want you to get away from me. I don't want to have to look at you all the time."

Clear enough? But he did it too masterfully, too well. Nearly swooning from the unexpected attention, heart all aflutter at having heard The Voice, Milly hastened to obey. If he ordered her to the very end of the line, that's where she went. But, the pleasurable effect soon wearing off, she was always drawn back again, hopeful of a repeat performance.

He could have gotten rid of her only by directing her to jump off a cliff.

During one layover, he became desperate enough to take her aside for a frank talk.

"See here," he protested roughly. "I am a steer."

"Yes, and what a steer!" Milly enthused, forgetting her maidenly reserve so far as to speak her first words to him.

That's as far as the discussion got.

After a couple of nights on the trail, the Herefords made adequate troops; their only fault lay in having doubled our numbers. Crossings of roads and streams, and negotiation of fences, took twice as long; and, for shelter in the daytime, just any old grove would not do. Now, when I found one large enough, we stopped, even if the hour was early, for there might not be another. Thus was our march slowed, which of course increased our exposure.

The first actual mischance occurred at a place called Lake Tschida, where I had forgotten about a dam the Two-Legs had thrown across the Heart.

This was a rude surprise to bump up against in the middle of a moonless night. So, too, were the campground — full up for the Labor Day weekend — and the dozens of cabins and trailer houses we sensationalized in our blind blundering around the ten-mile impoundment!

The result was a lot of low comedy and destruction of property. On the plus side, nobody — two legs or four — got hurt, and a semi-stampede does make for a snappy night's march. When we finally got ourselves reorganized, out of danger, everyone was accounted for. And I consoled myself that, even if we had left the lake in an uproar, the Two-Legs could scarcely have known what hit them. At that hour, anyone not groggy from sleep was probably tippling.

The newspaper accounts were confused, to be sure; but, taken with other oddities reported over the past week, made a pattern for anybody with the eyes to see.

First, rustlers were suspected of being at work in the Heart River country. (Far from having disappeared with the Old West, rustling has become motorized and taken to the highway.) There seemed no other explanation for the disappearance of fourteen or fifteen cattle from the scene of a derailment west of Mandan. Then, a few days later, a Hereford operator at Almont missed another dozen head.

Simultaneously, people were reporting strange sights along the Heart.

These involved a herd of "ghost cattle," led by a bull of mythic proportions, that came out only at night. The bull was variously described as black, as "shining white" (Duke?) and even — my favorite — *transparent*. The favored (though not invariable) direction of travel was west.

Someone suggested a connection between the ghost herd and the missing cattle, but the notion of rustlers conducting a trail drive across western North Dakota seemed too fantastic.

Bad enough that, unbeknownst to me, half the state was on the lookout for rustlers, phantom cattle or both. In addition, the law was at least mildly interested in a young man — not considered dangerous — who had pulled off a bold jailbreak in Fargo and was thought to have fled west in a stolen pickup.

* * *

Two days out from Lake Tschida, during our layover, I had the damnedest dream involving Counts the Coffee.

We were engaged in barehanded combat, a to-the-death struggle. Coffee was terrifically strong — who would have thought it? We tumbled and flailed, kicked and gouged, he on top one minute and I the next. Finally I had him on his back and my fingers around his fat throat! His eyes were all bugged out and could not blink away the blood dripping from my face onto his.

The dream was as real-seeming as that. Then my hands closed on themselves and he was gone — vanished! I couldn't believe it! I beat my fists on the ground and let out a yell of frustrated rage.

Here I awoke, much to the relief of Billy and my other neighbors, who had been forced to give my violent struggles plenty of room. I was all skinned up, and even took away a headache that persisted for hours.

I did not feel like talking about my dream, and Billy did me the favor of not asking. He had had plenty of experience with nightmares.

It was at the camp after this one that we learned of Billy's changed feelings toward Milly. He may have only discovered them for himself.

He and I were reviewing the previous night's march when a bawl of feminine distress reached our ears. Billy leapt right up and took off through the trees to investigate, I following with some others.

We discovered Duke herding Milly around and around a confined area of fallen and leaning trees, attempting — somewhat angrily — to mount her. Poor old Duke! — he had all of it on display, but it was in the wrong shape. To encourage himself, to help performance catch up with his best intentions, he was "talking dirty" — informing the scandalized Milly of what was going to take place any minute now.

"I can't hear a word you're saying!" she cried. "Help, somebody!"

Before I could take action, Billy tied into the old bull with everything he had, catching him by surprise and fairly staggering him. Nor did he stop there, following up with a second ferocious head butt — roaring all the while and throwing off lassos of foam.

Duke, doubly humiliated, was not to be kept off-balance for long. To interrupt a bull at his pleasure is not on the free list, even (or especially) if the pleasure has been more of a frustration. Fiddled-out or no, the oldster quickly had his legs under him again and must soon have given a good account of himself at Billy's expense, if I had not interposed myself.

"Take Milly and get out of here," I told Billy.

"Not until I've settled with Rag-Dick, here," he cried hotly. "Get out of my way!"

I was taking a pretty fair pummeling from both sides. I called to Wilbur and Ralph for help, and it was thanks to them that Billy and Milly were finally herded away. Then all I had to worry about was getting the Duker calmed down.

This took some doing. In his long life, nobody had trifled with him and walked away; at the same time, whipping me to get at Billy was not in the cards, and he knew it. To the accumulating evidence of waning hardihood had been added one more proof, and the shame of it was almost more than he could bear.

I excused my interference to him on the grounds that Billy was my second most-valuable lieutenant, after Duke himself; and that his destruction at Duke's hands — a foregone conclusion — would have been a crippling blow to the expedition. I asked his forgiveness for putting the general welfare first, at his expense.

Also: "You would be doing me a favor if you stayed away from Milly. It's evident that Billy feels protective of her, and you have all the other cows to choose from, from what I hear of their talk. They can't say enough about you!"

"It's true that the word is getting around," Duke harrumphed, so easily are we flattered out of our worst self-doubts. He was still sulky but ready to be mollified.

"As for the girl, I will give her up if you say. Anyway, she is not my type. She is flat-chested as an alligator."

Billy was easier, the firebrand of half an hour before having quite subsided.

"The fact is, I'm growing fond of Milly," he confessed. "But what right do I have to do that? Duke is right — the sooner she gets educated, the better. It would save everybody a lot of heartache over the long run. But how do I just watch her go to somebody else?"

Alas, I had no answer for that one — or for what I was supposed to do now instead of smile when the subject of Billy and Milly came up.

CHAPTER 25

"Halt!" came the challenge from out of the twilight, in a steer's voice. "You shall not pass!"

I could scarcely believe my ears. Oh, we had had our eye on them for some minutes, silhouetted against the cobalt sky and new moon: about twenty cattle lining the far bank of Antelope Creek. The only thought I had given them was to remind our soldiers of the rule — yes, we had one now — against fraternizing.

Billy and I were leading the way when the surprising order came.

"Who says so?" I demanded.

Cattle do have a keen territorial sense — just watch a herd turned into new pasture. They will wear themselves out exploring it, scarcely stopping to eat until they have gotten the feel of it. However, it is only the bull who is supposed to defend boundaries.

A steer stepped forward. "Maynard is my name," he said, "and I am the boss in these parts."

"Maynard!" Duke mocked, pushing to the front and spoiling for a fight.

"Just hold on," I told him. A determined opposition, if that is what we faced, could complicate our crossing, no doubt.

To the steer I said: "This is certainly a stroke of luck. Whenever I can, I like to get the boss's permission before crossing his land."

"You are not talking to a child," this Maynard said. "You can stow that stuff."

Inwardly, I had to smile. "Very well, Maynard, let's get down to cases. We are only passing through, not moving in on you. We propose to cross your creek and be on our way. We don't require so much as a blade of your grass."

He said, "Oh, I guess we know what you're up to, all right," and his companions murmured in agreement.

"You do?"

"Oh, yes," Maynard affirmed. "You are running away

from the Two-Legs — in fact, running for your lives. You are headed for the Badlands."

I was temporarily speechless.

"Far from blaming you," he continued mildly, "we would like to tag along. In fact, that is our price if you are to proceed yourselves. Being only human," he chuckled, "we do not want to go to the slaughterhouse either!"

Billy and I just looked at each other. Our people began stamping their feet nervously and lowing among themselves. Duke huffed and demanded of me:

"What is this business about a slaughterhouse? Does it have anything to do with head cheese?"

"What an ugly word!" exclaimed another. "I hate the very sound of it."

I finally recovered my tongue. "See here, Maynard. You and I must have a talk. Shall I come over?"

"I think not," he laughed. "We might not get you to go back again! No, I will come to you."

He was as careful as he was crafty, crossing with a considerable guard. With Duke and Billy, I led them downstream a little way, out of earshot of the others.

"Now," I said, "where did you get this story about us?"

Maynard's account, so simple and apparently straightforward, created more difficulties than it cleared up.

"A couple of days ago, a stranger appeared among us. He was a First People, like ourselves. He told us what you were doing and that we should be ready when you came along. He said" — Maynard's tone was reproachful — "you might not want our company."

"I would like to speak with this stranger," I said.

"Alas, that is impossible. He went on his way immediately — 'to alert our brothers and sisters up the river,' he said."

Who was this bovine Paul Revere? Even more vexing, what would we do about all the cattle he was rallying to intercept us?

In a huddle excluding Maynard, Billy surprised me by

agreeing with Duke that we must draw a line on additions. "We can beat them in a fight," he declared.

But Billy had infected me with his morality as I had infected him with mine. It seemed hardhearted to abandon this crowd to their fate, knowing what they did — groan as I might at the thought of doubling our numbers yet again.

"You may come," I told Maynard sternly. "But only on the condition that there is no more of this rubbish about a slaughterhouse. That is just scare talk with no foundation in fact. We are after freedom, nothing else. You must instruct your people."

"No slaughterhouse," Maynard said drily, bowing his head. "I will tell them."

A few hours later we arrived at the place where the Green River — which is quite small, more of a creek — drops its limpid waters into the Heart. Here, on an inspiration, I had us cross over and proceed up that.

Soon Maynard came running up from the rear.

"Surely our river goes the other way!" he exclaimed with some heat. "You have made a wrong turn!"

On the contrary, our debacle at Lake Tschida had sensitized me to modern geography; and I had been worrying ever since about our Heart River route, which shortly would pick up the railroad again, then require a sweeping detour around the city of Dickinson. How could I have forgotten our good old Green, which takes off northwest for the Badlands through a neighborhood much more secure?

An explanation was not owed Maynard but was tendered him anyway.

He chuckled low. "It also takes us out of the way of any more volunteers, isn't that right?"

"That entered into it," I replied. "Now kindly return to your people and see if you can't hurry them along a little."

"There is something about that one," Billy said. I was to hear similar sentiments from my other soldiers. I could see what they meant, for Maynard rubbed me the wrong way too; although I only thought him too smart by half.

The light of day showed our new charges to be of the Gelbvieh persuasion. Their red hides added to our rainbow look and also to the mystery surrounding their informant. As Billy pointed out, we had met up with no other "First People" — no Gelbviehs — on our route.

Splashing under the twin bridges of I-94, that night we met up with Maynard, I allowed myself to think of us as on the home stretch. To the best of my memory, we were all done with "the settlements" now, with only forty miles or so of nice lonesome country remaining before we tucked the Badlands around us like a blanket.

The next couple of nights and days were uneventful. Our change of course had fixed our numbers for good and all. We did run into more cattle, but — unalerted — they proved merely curious. We left them as we found them.

One new development was the inseparableness of Billy and Milly. Since her latest rescue at Billy's hands, the pretty heifer had become even more devoted in her attentions, while he had ceased to resent and shun them. In fact, on the trail and in camp, they were constantly at one another's side — talking little but exchanging frequently the kind of rapt, soulful looks that gave the name to "cow eyes."

"Look at that, will you?" Duke laughed — although the prettiness of their love had won him over to respect if not understanding.

At sunup following our third night on the Green, we went into camp at the prettiest place yet, an extensive stand of cottonwoods below a soaring butte. The peacefulness of the spot — the mature trees like the sails of a great ship, registering an otherwise-imperceptible breeze with a constant rustling sigh at their tops — would not last.

Our people had just begun "moving in," dispersing through the trees to seek forage, when Ralph sought me out, all worked up.

"There is a Two-Legs in the woods!"

This was a cruel trick to have played on us so near our goal and after we had survived so many hazards.

"A Two-Legs — only one?"

"Only one."

A fisherman, I thought, given the hour — unfortunately, one likely to know interlopers when he saw them.

"Show me," I said.

I was prepared for somebody already giving the alarm on a cell phone or otherwise mobilized for action. What I found was a pickup with a guy slouched behind the wheel regarding us lazily from under the brim of his cowboy hat. As we studied him, in turn, the fellow righted himself, pushed back his hat and laughed.

"Mav, you son of a gun!" he cried. "What are you doing out here? Have you come to finish me off, or what?"

I'd have known that red hair and lantern jaw anywhere. It was Red, the cowboy I had nearly killed last month in the Red River Valley!

CHAPTER 26

"Aw, it wasn't as bad as all that," said Red, as we got caught up beside his pickup. "You only knocked me out. Gave me a concussion, they say."

He laughed. "Truth to tell, I'm not a hundred percent yet. For one thing, I can talk to animals."

And could understand what we said back!

"I don't know what you do for a living now," I told him. "But I'd think there would be some handsome opportunities for you in veterinary medicine."

I asked what in the world he was doing in these woods, and he pinned that on the concussion too.

"They just wouldn't let me alone. I was going crazy in that hospital in Fargo, so I took off. My brother got worried and ratted me out to the sheriff. So then I had to pop a deputy. That earned me a trip to the county lockup, to their infirmary. Well, that was worse than the hospital, and I had to check myself out of there too. And here I am."

In his travels — in a "borrowed" truck — Red had picked up a *Tribune* that told of his flight. He seemed to get a kick out of the notoriety. I had to "ahem" and point out a brief on the same page concerning the rumored herd of ghost cattle.

Naturally, Red wanted to know what we thought we were doing — and, learning, liked the sound of the Badlands for himself.

"I can't eat grass, but I'll bet you what — I can live on deer meat and bullberries until the law forgets about this poor cowboy and goes back to chasing criminals."

His pickup had come furnished with a rifle and ammo that would help him live off the land. He proposed to abandon the truck itself and proceed with us on foot. "Or I could ride you," he joked.

"I believe that's been tried," I said.

Red had been observing our same routine of lying low by day and moving at night — when he moved. He had been in this spot for two days already, living off a stash of snack food. When I expressed surprise that, motorized, he had gotten no further, he said:

"Shit, I don't want to live nowhere but North Dakota. Why should I have to? I ain't done nothin' wrong."

By his lights, he hadn't — like me, I guess.

A column in the *Tribune* by my old friend Ed Advancing Along had caught my eye. Later, after Red and I were up to date, I treated myself as follows:

Bad ideas continue to hurt American prosperity and nudge people toward dependency and the government corral. Among them:

FREE TRADE. A collaboration of the best economic minds and both political parties, in only a generation free trade has hollowed out our manufacturing base and made keyboard punchers of our formerly skilled and broad-shouldered working folks.

Besides jobs, we ship overseas about $50 billion a month, net, the amount of our trade deficit — and have been doing so for thirty years.

China, the main beneficiary these days, turns our dollars into missiles pointed at us and our Asian friends.

AFFORDABLE HEALTH CARE. This is aimed at relief for people who make too much money to qualify for Medicaid but would rather spend it on electronics and restaurant meals than on insurance premiums.

An unforeseen consequence — which could have been foreseen by a differently abled baboon — is the effect of the employer mandate. Employers have sensibly responded by declining to take on new hires and by turning full-time jobs into part-time ones that do not come under the mandate.

MAN-MADE CLIMATE CHANGE. The holy war on carbon-based fuels destroys jobs, raises the price of everything and delivers us into the hands of OPEC — all in the name of suppressing carbon dioxide.

But what is this gnat against which we have mobilized the Strategic Air Command?

Carbon dioxide amounts to 400 parts per million of all gases in the atmosphere — less than one-half of 1 percent. This stays approximately constant, carbon dioxide having a half-life of ten years. Of the miniscule carbon-dioxide total, "this busy monster, manunkind," working as hard as he can, accounts for between 2 and 3 percent.

Bad ideas: Surveying their effects, all tending to less freedom and more government control, a suspicious person could be excused for wondering if bad ideas might not be ... the whole idea!

Later that morning, Billy and I went on reconnaissance, following a cattle trail up the easy side of the butte. (Red wanted to go too, but I persuaded him that two cattle up there in plain sight was one thing, a Two-Legs something else.)

The view from on top was extensive. My heart speeded up when I saw the broad band of conical hills to the west, no more than a good night's march away.

"There are your Badlands," I told Billy.

He seemed taken aback. "They are well-named," he said, after a pause.

The midday sun had drawn from them most of their color and all shadow relief, giving them an aspect white and rather severe. I assured Billy of the goodness awaiting discovery in their folds and defiles.

"Then you do think we can live there?" he said.

I had been weighing this question, especially since our original numbers had increased so dramatically. (We were now nearly fifty.) It was hard to imagine the ranchers and National Forest Service long overlooking such a crowd helping itself to their grass. There was also the winter to look forward to. We would be on our own, while the other cattle were getting fed. Maybe we would all starve.

"There is no guarantee," I said. "All we're doing out there is giving ourselves a chance."

I liked Billy's conclusion, after he had chewed on this for only a moment. "Which we did not have before," he said.

"Not a prayer," I agreed.

"Well, that's good enough for me."

"It's all I ask for myself."

CHAPTER 27

That afternoon a single-engine plane came droning up the valley, flying low. I thought I knew what that meant, but there was nothing to be done. With the lonesomeness of the country I had grown more relaxed in the matter of concealment, and probably half of us were in sight outside the woods. Still, cattle in cattle country were, by themselves, blameless; it all depended on who was in the plane and if he realized what he was looking at.

The plane brushed us with its shadow, lowered its voice and passed on up the river.

Ralph laughed in relief and was reminded of a story about a pair of calves and their first experience of a similar plane.

"That is surely the largest bird I have ever seen," said one, as the craft sputtered overhead.

"Yes, indeed," replied the other. "And we'd better mind our heads, for it sounds like he has been in the wild fruit."

Red was less sanguine. He knew how close we were to the Badlands and wanted to make a run for it.

I vetoed that — there were too many hours of daylight left. If the Two-Legs were on to us, we'd never make it; if they weren't, there was no necessity.

Red grumbled, then settled down for a suspenseful wait. For a couple of hours I entertained the wishful thought we were only waiting for dark. Then the westering sun began glancing off something — motor vehicles, as it turned out, slowly moving our way out of the glare, cross-country down the valley.

"We're screwed like a tied-up housecat," Red growled. "I told you we should have high-tailed it."

One at a time our soldiers joined us on the edge of the woods to watch the caravan's dusty progress. I missed Red for a minute, and when he rejoined us, he was toting his rifle.

"What do you think you're going to do with that?" I asked.

He was already "loaded and locked." Red looked at me

with some impatience. "We can't let them just waltz in," he said.

He made me realize we had two different problems here. "You're in enough trouble with the law as it is," I said.

"And you're only going to the slaughterhouse," Red laughed.

"There's that word again," Duke rumbled. "I want to know about this slaughterhouse."

"No, you don't, pard," Red said absently. Then, to me: "But what are you getting at, Mav?"

"Well, I think you ought to give yourself up," I said.

Red was incredulous. "Give up!" he cried. "Is that what you're going to do?"

Of course I had to admit that, for the rest of us, surrender was not in the cards. Whereupon Red asked me to look more closely at his own situation.

"They've already got me for assaulting a peace officer and resisting arrest," he said. "Since then, I've broken out of jail, and I can just see them claiming I stole that truck.

"Now I've got you guys hanging around my neck. They're going to call me a rustler too!"

I will admit the rustling angle hadn't occurred to me. Red proceeded to get worked up, for him.

"That would be worth five or ten years by itself! Or, wait — maybe I could clear myself by calling you as a witness. Then they'd only send me to the funny farm, instead!"

He was breathing hard from the injustice of it all.

"Okay," I said, but made him promise he wouldn't shoot anybody.

"I'm not a fool," he said, and grinned. "They don't need to know that, though."

Indeed, I'm sure our visitors didn't know what they were dealing with. Their plane may or may not have seen Red or his pickup; in any case, they did not "waltz in" as if they were only rounding up some cattle. Rather, they drew up their half-dozen vehicles a hundred yards away, on the other side of the river, and just sat for a few minutes.

Two or three of the vehicles looked "official," the others not. We would see more of both kinds over the next day as local residents joined law enforcement in the standoff.

The sheriff let us wait a while before getting on his bullhorn, and then he was unexcited, even friendly, welcoming us to his county.

"I do have some business to talk over with you," he continued, "if you'd be good enough to come out and head over this way."

I thought we needed to say something to confirm we amounted to more than cattle in here.

"Go pound salt!" Red bellowed, through cupped hands.

You could almost see the sheriff smiling and shaking his head.

"You boys have it your way," he said mildly. "We can wait."

I liked that 'boys' — if he thought we were more than just Red, so much the better. But I could take only so much comfort in the unlikelihood, at least for now, of a charge on the woods. Before nightfall, our visitors had moved in all the comforts of home, including a couple of portable toilets, a generator and lights. About their staying power there could be no doubt.

Worst of all, for Red, as the sun went down, were the cooking smells wafting from the camp.

"The son of a bitches are frying steak!" he cried. "No offense," he excused himself, to me.

In our larder was a little poor grass in the woods, which was of no use to Red, and not much better outside, the pasture having had a summer of hard use. Maynard, the Gelbvieh, dropped by to inquire of me "where you think this thing is going."

"If you have a plan, I think we deserve to hear it," he said. "If not, maybe we ought to see if the Two-Legs will give us something to eat."

Some of our people within earshot murmured agreement, already forgetful of what their nights on the trail had been for. To Maynard Billy bristled: "We took you on out of charity.

You're along for the ride — you do not call the shots!"

All I could offer — to Maynard and anybody else who asked — was the vision, again, of the free life in the Badlands.

"That's worth holding out for — not surrendering until there is no other way. And we're not at that point yet."

I stopped short of saying, "Something might turn up." That sounded too forlorn, even if it did comprise the whole of my poor "plan." Indeed, it was hard to imagine the circumstances that would allow us to run the roadblock that had been put in our way and then outrace it to the Badlands!

CHAPTER 28

It was a long restless night in the woods, seemingly endless, the crickets ringing tirelessly, the half-moon taking forever to work its way down the sky. Our people couldn't sleep for hunger, and kept slipping down to the river to fill up on water. The baby calves could tap their mamas, but occasionally one of the adults would forget himself and let slip a bawl of complaint.

I'm pleased to say this usually brought a 'shush' of reproach from somebody, with the offender, in turn, usually having the good grace to apologize.

Between these disturbances and a shift I took on watch, I got little sleep. At sunup, I was dropping off for a nap when I was roused by Red's excited shout.

"Somebody stole my rifle!" he cried. He had left it behind long enough to go relieve himself, and missed it on his return.

My first confused thought was that we must have been raided by someone from the sheriff's camp. But, if so, shouldn't he have taken the opportunity to get the drop on us — on Red — by now? I tried to clear the cobwebs.

"You didn't misplace it?" I asked, a suggestion Red emphatically denied.

A couple of Gelbvieh steers stood nearby, chewing placidly on something — the memory of yesterday's grass, perhaps. I asked if they had seen anything, and tried to recall for them Red's gun.

After some tail-switching thought, one of them spoke up. "The stranger took it," he said.

"Maynard," said the other.

Maynard, 'the stranger' — which was it? Red asked, more to the point, "Where did he go with it?"

This was answered for us by the 'crack' of a gun coming from riverside, followed by a bellow of pain. Red and I took off running through the trees and brush.

"I'd step kind of careful on the other side of that bush," Red prompted.

We burst out of the trees onto the beach. In the new pink-orange sunlight, Maynard stood beside the water, hindquarters sagging, cussing fluently. Another moment, and he sat all the way down, on his haunches, as a dog would. Nearby stood Billy, Red's rifle dangling from his jaws.

Red retrieved the gun, freeing up Billy's mouth.

"He was going to throw it in the river," Billy said.

Maynard complained, "The bleeping expletive shot me in the bleeping ass."

Billy explained it as an accident as they struggled for possession of the gun. "If I had shot him on purpose, it would have been between the eyes," he said.

All on his own, Billy had been keeping an eye on Maynard and had seen him make off with the gun.

The Gelbvieh steers had followed us onto the beach. I asked the first one, "Why, back there, did you call him a stranger?"

He told a bewildering story of how Maynard, a formerly placid sort, had had a kind of fit one day and emerged from it with an altogether different personality — overbearing and evangelical.

"He's the one who told us you were coming and we must prepare to follow. Where he got that, we didn't know. Everybody thought he was crazy, and was afraid of him. Then you showed up, just as he had said."

So Maynard himself was the mysterious messenger of whom he had told us! It was a companion evangel (and fit-thrower), the Gelbvieh said, who had proceeded up the Heart to organize more cattle yet on our line of march.

By now we had been joined by my other soldiers. I was worried that the sheriff might take advantage of our confusion to make a move on us, but his camp — in plain view — appeared quiet. It turned out they were as enthralled as we, with not only field glasses turned on us but cameras out of television stations in Dickinson and Bismarck.

Maynard continued in his sitting posture. The wound, in the fleshy part of his right hip, did not look serious, but you wouldn't have known it from his bellyaching.

"It's stiffening up," he whined. "I won't be able to walk."

I said: "You weren't going anyplace anyway — or planning to let the rest of us go, either. You might as well explain yourself, for your little game is up. Who are you — really?"

"I can't move. Give me a drink of water, and maybe I'll tell you," Maynard said.

"Speak up this minute, and maybe we won't shoot you," I replied.

"You asked for it," Maynard said.

With that, he rolled his eyeballs back on a fire dancing in his skull, flames darting out of the sockets like tongues! Simultaneously, his lips opened like a hideous black flower, showing all his teeth, and he regarded us with a death's-head grin, a silent scream.

"You know me now," he said at last. "Don't you?"

CHAPTER 29

Counts the Coffee had lost none of his showman's flair, and he achieved his effect, quite staggering all of us. Even the bluff Red and Duke were struck dumb. However, when my own wits began to creep back, I realized I was looking at, if not a broken man, one who had been, since our last meeting, considerably reduced.

Coffee settled down quickly enough, following his little theatrical flourish, and my surmise that there had been a shakeup in the HHG was borne out by the story he had to tell.

"You've been making the newspapers," he said sourly. "I didn't realize the Old Man even read them anymore, except to find out where Marty Stuart or Ricky Skaggs was playing.

"You caught his eye, anyway, with your rodeo shenanigans — especially the beer drinking. (Me, I recognized you right off the bat, in that affair with the picnic basket.) I wish he'd said something at the time — I could have been better prepared. But I think it was only when you started making off with all these cattle — got half the state in an uproar — that he really woke up."

The Great Spirit took Coffee by surprise, cutting a trip short and arriving home unexpectedly.

"I was making myself at home at his place, as I liked to do," Coffee said, and shook his head. "I'm afraid I had my feet up on his desk! He came storming in, thrust a newspaper in my face and demanded to know what the hell was going on in Dispatching."

Coffee seemed in awe at the memory yet.

"He insisted on seeing your old file, the one from Fort Clark. He asked for it by name, 'Black Bull Medicine.' Don't ask me how he knew exactly what he was looking for. It's what he does, I guess."

He sighed. "So I had to cough it up. We're all-electronic now, and it was a matter of a few mouse clicks. Well, he just went through the roof! Then, while he was at it, he had to nose into some of my other files — my 'Greatest Hits,' if you like. From bad to worse!

"Honestly, I've never seen anybody get so mad — it was really quite impressive. You know, I always thought the Old Man was kind of a puss. It turns out that everything they say about his anger is true! The fact is, he scared the living shit out of me."

Which was by way of explaining Coffee's present business. According to him, the Great Spirit's position was: "You dealt this mess, and now you will get down there and straighten it out, by God!"

Or words to that effect.

"And how were you supposed to do that?" I asked.

That word 'mess' — whether originating with the Great Spirit or only with Coffee — made me wary. I considered that I had a lot of credit coming for exposure of Coffee in his low dealing, and was prepared to resent at this point interference in my affairs by even the Great Spirit.

Coffee said, "By making you give yourself up."

"Give myself up? To whom?"

"Why, to the Two-Legs, of course."

I was outraged, fairly spluttering. Coffee only laughed. Indeed, it was at this point that he recovered some of his old swagger and insolence.

"The Old Man is resigned by now to humans getting too big for their britches," he said. "But he's not about to lose all control and watch the lower orders follow suit! Of course you're expected to surrender — start acting like a proper animal!"

All the way to the slaughterhouse, I thought bitterly.

"That's the thanks I get," I said, "for blowing up your little playhouse for him. Well, you and he can both forget it. The Two-Legs might get me in the end — but not because I quit!"

Coffee purred: "We never considered anything so unlikely of success as an appeal to reason.

"After we talked it over, we got on the Old Man's TV and found you in camp beside the Heart. You were sleeping at the time. The idea was for me to dispatch myself into your body and simply take you over. The old 'possession' bit, right?

"You may recall our little wrestling match."

Indeed I did — my 'nightmare' of a few days past!

"I would have won, if you weren't such a dirty fighter," Coffee said. "You hit me below the belt."

I would not dignify this lie with a response.

He went on: "The Old Man was not happy when I came limping back! But I had picked your brain and learned your plans. Soon I had another idea.

"We used the TV again to pan on up the river until we found some more cattle — the Gelbviehs! A friend and I jumped two of them and took them over easily. (They didn't fight dirty.) Then it was simply a matter of our preparing the others to intercept you.

"We were going to add to your numbers until you were too many, too big, to hide any longer. I stayed with the Gelbviehs to deal with you, to make sure you took us on. My friend proceeded up the Heart to continue recruiting.

"And that's about it, my friend."

I was a minute in putting my finger on something that bothered me about his story — something besides the malodorous collusion between the Great Spirit and himself to bring me to heel. Seeing me lost in thought, and growing impatient, Coffee wheedled:

"And now, my friend, if you will honor your promise. Such long telling has left me drier than ever. A drink of water, if you would be so kind."

And then I had it.

"Coffee! Can it be you never considered defying your orders and throwing in with us — helping us on our way instead of hurting us?"

He gave me an uncomprehending look, and I had to lay it out for him.

"Consider your situation. You're washed up in the Happy Hunting Ground. Down here, you had nothing to look forward to, after your dirty work was done, but the — you know, the same thing the rest of us were looking at."

I had come that close to saying the forbidden word.

I continued: "Don't tell me you never thought, 'These people may have something going for themselves. Why shouldn't I go with them to the Badlands and breathe free air, be my own man?' "

Coffee shook his head emphatically.

"Not for a minute," he said. "Life down here is short in any case. The Happy Hunting Ground is forever. And the Old Man is getting forgetful. Who knows? If I do this job for him, maybe over time he'll forget all about that — other stuff. It's my best bet, in any case."

I might have known. It was all about the path of least resistance — the sure thing, the old featherbed.

Our entire conversation must have been bewildering to everybody else. Billy, Duke and their mates couldn't have comprehended the half of it — but Red had picked up enough to form a rough idea.

"I say we do him a favor and send him on his way right now," he said, ejecting the spent cartridge from his rifle and bolting the new into place.

Coffee shrank, coward that he was, but I stayed Red's hand — don't ask me why. Maybe I only thought Coffee deserved to drag himself around on that bum leg for a while.

"A bullet is too good," I said, and reviewed for Coffee what I thought of him, brought up to date for current events.

"You were right in character again, destroying the peace of mind of the Gelbviehs and who knows how many others, planning all the time to sabotage the deliverance you promised them.

"That was cruel even for you. To get any lower, you'd have to dig a hole. But even I wasn't prepared for one so abject that he preferred" — and again I caught myself — "going to market himself to freedom in the Badlands. (Although I'm sure you'd be bawling for mercy at the end and soiling yourself!)

"If I had understood this about you, I never would have called you the wickedest of men but the most miserable — with the power to enslave others but not to free yourself."

Coffee had been shaken by Red's threat, as described. Now he stared at the ground for a silent interval, pretending to be ashamed. When he finally raised his eyes, he tried to look almost as wretched as I had made him out, and said in a very small voice:

"Does this mean I don't get my water?"

I had never actually promised him any such thing, but in the end I had Red give it to him anyway, out of his hat. Coffee was incorrigible — and through bad and worse I had known him for more than two hundred years.

CHAPTER 30

We were only beginning a day of extraordinary events.

Billy, of course, had the full expression of my gratitude for preserving our only weapon and the deterrent option. Indeed, as the story got around, he became the toast of the woods. We needed something to celebrate; there was next to nothing to eat, and it was getting harder to imagine a happy ending to the standoff.

Certainly the sheriff and his posse were going nowhere. The sheriff kept it friendly, getting on his horn to ask what we were having for breakfast.

"We've got plenty," he said, "if you'd like some of ours."

We could smell their preparations, right enough, and they did make Red cuss again. "I wish I had that growler back," he said.

As the sun climbed higher on our second day in the woods, and the temperature rose, our people lay about here and there, conserving their strength. In one group, Ralph was seeking to entertain from his store of jokes and riddles.

Q: Why is the sunflower the most-American flower?
A: Because it's always on the road.

Then Counts the Coffee came dragging up. Yes, he was on his feet already, limping around and making a great show of his suffering. He listened for a time, then interjected:

"I've got one. How long can you go without eating before it's time for the crows to start eating you?"

Again, it was only I who saved him from an impulsive bullet from Red. I banished Coffee to riverside in the charge of Wilbur and put him out of my mind. I had enough to think about otherwise. I detached myself from the company and undertook a solitary walk to try again for a fresh approach.

I had not gone far when another distraction presented itself. From behind some bushes in my path came the unmistakable sounds by which lovemaking announces its final frenzy.

Bemused, thinking the Duker must be enjoying a refreshment of his prime, and not wishing to disturb, I stopped

132

in my tracks. Before I could detour — decently withdraw — the business was finished, the bushes parted and out stepped Milly!

I was thunderstruck, heartsick, at the grossness of this betrayal. Granted, the day must come when she took a proper partner; but this was too soon — a coldblooded abandonment of the sweetness of childish love.

Milly drew up short, looking startled and embarrassed. This gave her consort the opportunity to catch up, and I was shaken again. The face pushing through the bushes was not Duke's but Billy's!

Tell me it couldn't have happened, accuse me of grossly implausible fictioneering, and I will cite you examples from history of harem-tending eunuchs who were foxes in the henhouse, of Italian *castrati* singers who could still manage a low note.

In Billy's case, I think the explanation is love, plain and simple. Milly helped him find the parts he was missing, and they were mystically restored to him. (His lionization of that morning for stopping Coffee can't have hurt.)

Excusing myself, I beat a hasty retreat. But it did not take Billy long to look me up. It was not for the purpose of boasting — although there was a new swagger to his walk — but to outline a bold plan for breaking the sheriff's blockade and getting us on our way.

"When it gets dark, I will cross the river and charge their camp," he said. "When I have thrown it into perfect confusion, the rest of you can start up the river on this side. I will rejoin you later, on the trail."

I recognized a dangerous euphoric phenomenon from the old days, when one of us young Mandan bucks, full of testosterone and dreams of glory, would propose some outrageous stroke against the enemy, the riskier the better. We would say it was *a good day to die*.

The old Billy was all the way back — and I credit him with shaking me out of the unconscious torpor into which I

133

had fallen. Action — if not his exact proposal, some variation of it — was essential, and soon. As it was, under my non-leadership, we were lying around until we should run out of calories and flight of any kind be impossible.

I burned with the realization that we should have been off last night already!

Accordingly, I called a war council that had the immediate benefit of energizing everybody.

It was decided that Billy and I would tackle the sheriff's camp together — reminiscent of the old days at the Dolans'! — with Red assuming leadership on the trail at least until we could catch up. (Red was even armed with a pair of wire cutters, out of the toolbox in the back of his pickup.)

There was just a chance that, in stampede mode — as at Lake Tschida — and with the aid of darkness we could evade and outrun the Two-Legs, making the Badlands in the one night!

CHAPTER 31

The following hours passed quickly as we refined our strategy. Then, in late afternoon, we heard from our friendly sheriff — in a manner of speaking.

There was a crackle in his bullhorn this time, and we could hardly make him out. "Did you get that?" I asked Red.

"I think they want to parley," he said, taking up his rifle. "I heard something about 'Mary.' You don't think they'd send a girl?"

I had understood as imperfectly as Red; but several of us showed ourselves on the river side, above the beach where Coffee and Wilbur were. We watched a Jeep detach itself from the camp after a while and start our way out of the westering sun. As it bucked along, top down, over the rough ground, we made out a driver and that was all.

"As long as there's nobody hiding in back, scrunched down," Red said. "They'd better play it straight."

The driver drew up opposite us on the other bank, shut down and got out. He was a tall fellow, and dark, not in uniform; at the same time, he wasn't dressed like one of the locals, either, but in sports attire, along with western hat and boots. He held the lapels of his jacket open to show he was concealing no weapon.

"Can I come across?" he called.

"What do you say?" Red asked me.

"Tell him to come ahead."

The Green is narrow and shallow enough here that, with the help of a couple of stepping stones, he barely got his boots wet. As he labored up our bank, I realized I was looking at an American Indian and, moreover, a face I ought to know.

Another instant and I had it — this was the same mug that had looked back at me for years from the opinion page of one newspaper or another. I got all light in the head as I tried to divine the meaning of its owner's appearance here.

"That's far enough," Red said, while keeping his gun

pointed toward the ground. The man stopped twenty feet away and studied our little group with a half-smile, looking from one face to another.

"Ask him," I mooed to Red, "if his name is Advancing Along." For I could hardly believe my eyes yet.

"Advancing Along?" Red inquired. "What the hell kind of name is that?"

But he did as I requested, and now it was our visitor's turn to be surprised. "Why, yes," he said. "I'm him, too."

Before I could wonder at the meaning of that 'him, too,' he let drop the crusher.

"And you," he said, looking straight at me now. "Do I have the distinction of addressing my old friend, Black Bull Medicine?"

I rushed him, roaring. Anybody else would have run for his life, but Advancing Along only laughed and took a couple of steps to meet me — as if recognizing my crude attempt to pronounce the last name of my old confidante from another world, none other than Meriwether Lewis!

He clapped me on the shoulder; I cuffed him with my head. "It could have been nobody else but you!" he cried.

I was to learn that Lewis had been following my adventures from afar going back to Fort Clark and the picnic basket. "The locale, taken with your new persona, was strongly suggestive," he said later.

From late summer and my exploits on the rodeo circuit, he thought he knew his man for sure, and had even flown in once from back East. But that was just in time to be too late: I had just shipped out from Glen Ullin. After that, he depended on contacts at *The Bismarck Tribune* to keep him up to date. Learning from them that I was pinned down here, he bought another plane ticket.

How we talked, laughed and shed tears, until Red — on whom, of course, I depended for making myself understood — was nearly worn out.

"You, a black bull," Lewis kidded, pointing a finger. "That

tells me, if I didn't already know by other signs, that our old friend Counts the Coffee is still in business!"

I had not yet had time to bring him up to date on that subject.

"You should have seen yourself about thirty-five years ago," I countered. "You were no very promising sight in your cradle, I'll tell you."

"Nor for a good many years thereafter," he said, his look darkening. "Know all about that, do you? Well, that devil made it as hard on both of us as he could. Maybe we'll have the opportunity to thank him one day!

"But, if you'll excuse me for a minute, there's some business I must attend to."

So saying, Lewis extracted a cell phone from his pocket and placed a call. The conversation was short and, at his end at least, cryptic enough, evidentally in some kind of code. "The stars are out," or something similar, is one of the things he said.

"Washington, D.C.," he told us, with a great air of mystery. "In a minute they'll be ringing up your governor, who is standing by and prepared, in turn, to get hold of your Bureau of Criminal Investigation."

Whatever that was, I would have wished my old friend more clear about the relevance of all this to ourselves and our situation. But Lewis, in character with his previous self in the HHG, was as much of a showman, in his way, as Counts the Coffee, and not to be rushed.

"Something should be happening up at the sheriff's very soon," he dropped, by way of a hint, causing us to turn our attention that way. In no more than five minutes, which Lewis filled with somewhat self-conscious small talk, the camp was in motion, giving signs of — could it be? — breaking up!

Another ten minutes, and the first dust trails were retreating up the valley.

"How did you do that?" I demanded, through Red.

"I'll explain later," Lewis said. "Meanwhile, have you and

your party had enough of walking? If you're going anywhere in particular, I'd be happy to get on the phone again and see about a ride for everybody."

His look sought as plainly as words to learn if I was suitably impressed.

I was, I was — even as I thought the showing off was in danger of getting one-sided. As it happened, I had something to spring on Lewis too.

"That would be very welcome," I said. "As would some eats all around, as long as you're waving your magic wand."

Red garnished his translation with a brilliant smile and enthusiastic nods.

"First, though," I said, "if you would accompany me down this way, onto the beach. There is somebody down there I think you would like to see!"

CHAPTER 32

Lewis — Advancing Along — represents himself as belonging to "a freedom-loving group, amounting to a shadow government," that lends support to good causes that might otherwise be lost.

Convincing his associates that a ragtag bunch of strayed cattle made one of those causes was characterized by him as "my hardest sell." But he got the job done, raising the cash with which to buy our freedom from our former owners.

Easy, by comparison, was making Red's legal problems go away.

Lewis' last coup was the strings he pulled with the U.S. Forest Service to get us a piece of the million acres of grass it administers in the Badlands.

"They owe me big-time," Lewis explained. "I've located several of Clark's and my old campsites for them in Montana, all verifiable by the latest dating tools. They're thrilled to death, even if they don't know how I do it. I tell them right out I used to be Meriwether Lewis, and they just laugh."

In the Badlands we enjoy a good and free life in surroundings of austere beauty. We're not hiding out: You can even see us from time to time, if you're in the right place.

I hasten to say there is no welfare to it. Before his concussion healed and he lost the ability to converse with us, Red took dictation of my memoirs, the which you now hold in your hands. Proceeds from the sale of my book satisfy our grazing fee to the Forest Service and cover other expenses, such as hay in the winter and my subscription to *The Bismarck Tribune*.

Red is on the payroll as our business manager.

By the second year there was enough money for me to realize a cherished project: purchase of Mother from the Dolans.

Yes, Mother is with me again. Poor dear, her mind was all in a whirl at first, and I can't honestly say she knew me. I tried to instruct her in everything I thought she needed to remember, which only confused her further. My fault: She didn't need all that stuff. Once her loving heart had a chance to take over, it was as if we had never been apart. Now she thinks she has always lived in the Badlands.

Billy and Milly, Ralph, Wilbur — all are in place. The Duker continues to age as ungracefully as you would expect. Counts the Coffee? We did bring him with us, Lewis and I being unwilling to loose him on the world unsupervised.

The free life did not agree with him at first. He is no better a steer than he was a man, but out here he couldn't solve the problem of how to be a really *bad* steer. His attempts to organize his fellow cattle simply fell flat — he had nothing to offer that they didn't already have.

So, for the first couple of months Coffee limped around on that game leg of his and did nothing but bitch. The higher things in life holding no charm for him, he was in danger, I think, of actually dying of boredom or despair.

Coming to his rescue finally was that love of food that distinguished him both at Fort Clark and in the HHG. Turning to it with a sincerity and singleness of purpose that would be inspiring directed almost anywhere else, today Coffee is the fattest thing on three and a half legs and probably tips the scale at a ton or better.

The Great Spirit should have no trouble keeping an eye on him when he gets Coffee back next time.

Red brings us our hay and will just drop by, the rest of the year, to hang out. He is always armed with beer, and we have a good old time. I've trained myself to write him short notes on the legal pad he keeps in his truck for that purpose.

These slobbery scribblings must suffice for Lewis' rarer visits, as well. But, then, Lewis is full of enough chat for both of us, as you would look for in a newspaper columnist.

He keeps me up to date on his group's various freedom projects, which he sometimes sees as a losing battle, given the growing acceptance by Americans — even their expectation — of more nanny government all the time.

"Why not?" Lewis cries theatrically. "The welfare state has diminished freedom and ruined prosperity everywhere else it's been tried. Why would we not want it for ourselves?"

Then he laughs and recalls that, in Cold War days, he was just as gloomy about the seemingly inevitable triumph of the Soviet Union.

"Resist!" he concludes stoutly. "Never give up!"

Bless his heart, I couldn't have said it better myself. My very sentiments — yours too, I trust.

THE END

SPREAD THE BULL

Additional copies of BULL may be
purchased online at

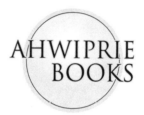

www.ahwipriebooks.com

or by mail from:
Ahwiprie Books
P.O. Box 2673
Bismarck, N.D. 58502

Books are $14.99, postpaid ($24.99 outside the U.S.)